BLACKJACK BRANNIGAN

(THE MONTANA SERIES)

L.J. MARTIN

WOLFPACK
PUBLISHING
— EST 2013 —

Blackjack Brannigan
(The Montana Series)

Paperback Edition
Copyright © 2019 L.J. Martin

Wolfpack Publishing
6032 Wheat Penny Avenue
Las Vegas, NV 89122

wolfpackpublishing.com

Paperback ISBN 978-1-64119-591-1
eBook ISBN 978-1-64119-590-4

BLACKJACK
BRANNIGAN

CHAPTER 1

GRUEL, AGAIN.

Oats, or some damn thing, cooked with too much water—now a gray slop—and a fist-size chunk of hard bread that's so damn wiggly with weevils it looks alive when it's just sitting on the hard, cold, stone floor. I wonder, are weevils good as meat? That's breakfast and with luck, lunch is beans that Cookie waved some bacon over, and it in a tin plate with only fifteen minutes to lean your pick or shovel aside so as to suck it down.

Thanks be to the good Lord I have a plan to put miles between me and Deer Lodge Prison. I figure seven years of a life sentence is enough for any man. And I've sure as hell become a man since they wrongly threw me in this hole only four months after I'd reached my majority of two years less than a score. And in this prison thanks be to who I thought was a friend, one who actually did the dirty deed I am imprisoned for, and his mine-owning, rich, son-of-a-she-dog daddy who owns not only a producing gold mine but also the judge and most the jury.

Beards and long hair are discouraged in the prison as lice are always a problem. Nonetheless, I now have two inches of face hair and my locks are to my shoulders. The greater chance that those on the outside who knew me as clean-shaven-and-nicely-combed will not recognize the older and much hairier me—should I live to confront them.

At eighteen, I wasn't the youngest in Deer Lodge, but I was damn sure the toughest for my years. It's a damn good thing I had my growth when I lit here as these big Indians, outlaws, and hooligans who keep me company would have used me badly had I not had rock-hard fists and the will to kick and bite like a mule. And been as hard headed as one.

Didn't take long to learn to fight like a mean old Jack donkey—fist, head-butt, kick, gouge, elbow, knee and teeth—but today is my day to scamper like a thorough-bred racehorse. And I plan to as they're taking us far up into the Flint Mountains to work a mine that I'd bet a dollar our crooked Warden Pickens has invested in—likely with money saved by feeding us gruel twice a day rather than meat and beans. Why else would Montana state prisoners be called upon to work a private holding?

Guard Titus Gradovich is as fair a man as hangs his hat in the guard shack of Deer Lodge, and I've made friends with him over these years by doing his bidding and not giving him fits like many other prisoners. And Titus has been as good to me as a guard could be expected to be. In fact, he was called to task by the warden for allowing me a free rein in the kitchen. He even allowed me to be alone from time to time when I had pot scrubbin' duty. And each time I was left to my own designs, I managed to slice a couple of thin strips of beef off the guard's grub, which I dried in the sun for jerky, then stowed in my thin mattress until I had more than a pound of vittles that would allow me three or four days of running without having to hunt a stomach full. I also had two pockets full of dried apple slices, apples meant for pies for guard and warden—pies always a few slices short but not enough to notice.

I'm as ready as I'll ever be. And what the hell are they gonna do to me if'n I'm caught? They'll throw me in the hole for a month or more for the attempt. But, hell, I'm in for life as it is, so what's a month in the hole on bread and water? This lousy gruel I'm finishing up ain't much better.

I've spent these seven years learning lots of things. For more than three years, one of my four cellmates was Blackfeet Pete Stealshorse, and I picked Pete's brain nearly every day about how the Indian survives in the Montana mountains and plains. I worked beside him on the outside, busting and shaping stone that was sold by the state to masons for construction, and took note of every bug and grub he munched down on, every mushroom he ate and those he called toadstools and shied from, every root he pulled and gnawed on and those he said were good for stomach aches or coughs or whatever. Pete's daddy was a medicine man, and he'd passed on lots of wood lore most white men would never know—but I did.

I've also spent these seven years gnawing on a hate that helped sustain me. That hate for them who wrongly got me put away for life was made worse when it came to me that my pa had died from consumption and my ma was forced to become a pleasure lady, then only last year died hard of the pox. I plan to wreak vengeance on those who put me here.

Colonel Maximillian Harrington is number one on my list; and his son Horace, number two. The judge who rapped the gavel and sent me up, Mortimer Allenthorp, was a circuit type and only knew what lies were laid out for him. Sheriff Anthony Papadopoulos was one whose palm the Harrington's crossed with gold, as was his deputy, Morgan Tuttle. Like the judge, I'd guess most of the jury to have been bamboozled by the Harringtons and Papadopoulos. All but Cornelius Caphorn, owner of the biggest saloon in Granite, a gold and silver town just on the other side of the Flint Mountains from the Deer Lodge Valley and this stone slammer. Most don't know it, but Harrington's a majority partner in Hard Rock Harry's. Corny and I have a date, soon as I square up with the other four. If you can call sending them to hell squaring up. Sounds square to me.

My current three cellmates have no idea I'm about to give escape a try. Mouse McNutt is a little guy who I would confide in were I needing someone to slip twixt the bars, which he's so skinny and pointy-headed he likely could do, but that's not my plan. Orval Peabody is a con man and could talk a toothless man out of his dentures in trade for a sack of walnuts, but talk won't get me over the mountains so he, too, has not been apprised of my plans. Jasper Todd Jefferson could be of use, and he's a fair man who I've come to be fond of, but he's due to finish his sentence of eight years in only two more. Jasper is built like a bull with a neck the size of my thigh that starts under his ears and flairs out from there. His back is crisscrossed with scars from being on the wrong end of a cat o' nine tails, and one ear is nipped off the top inch from the whip—and he'd likely go with me should I ask. We've been pals and have played a hundred or more games of checkers. But a white man and a black running together would be too easily spotted. So, I've not confided in Jasper. Pete Polkinghorn is well into his fourth score of years—oldest man in Deer Lodge at eighty some—and merely waiting to die. Every day he prays for forgiveness for chopping his wife to pieces. I have not befriended Pete and know no one who has. He's silent as his dead and dismembered spouse.

Rather than eat my fist-sized chunk of hard bread, I've pocketed it, along with the lid of a peach tin. Eight feet of cord surrounds my waist and my pocket holds three inches of steel bar that I hope will serve to spark a flint. A rock I hope to find in the Flint Mountains. If so, I'll have the makings of a fire. The tin lid will do for shavings, the steel and flint for sparks, and the cord as a snare for a fat snowshoe rabbit should I get lucky. I also have a dozen feet of catgut I purloined from the prison hospital and a two-inch length of wire that will work for a fish hook. I've been dreaming of roasting a fat lake trout over a bed of coals and eating it slathered in watercress from the streamside.

Fat Freddy Willard is the other kind of guard, who'd use a bludgeon on you if a kind word would do better, and it's him who rings the bell and yells out. "Them assigned to the Balls of Fire Mine get to the wagons. Eight to each. Brannigan," he snarls my name, "you drive the lead. Jasper you whip up number two. I'll drive three. Your tools is waitin' up there. Get your asses moving."

Willard will drive the last wagon, his Winchester at his side. That wagon holds a few tools, some buckets, our miserable lunch, and little else. He'll not have prisoners at his back, and I don't blame him for that as he's despised. Many would love the chance to slip up on him, cut his head off and pee down his neck hole.

Eighteen of us will be in front of him in two oar wagons, each pulled by a four up of mules flanked by two horseback guards. One guard we know by Red—Mister Red—as if you don't address a guard as Mister you're likely to get your head knotted the first time and the solitary hole the second. The other is O'Toole, with the small ears and mouth of an Irishman. He's rumored to be a sodomizer and known to be a rotten son-of-a-bitch. He once tried his charms on me resulting in his eyebrow needing ten catgut stitches, and me pleased to spend a month in the hole on bread and water for the offense.

It was worth it.

We'll ride the nine miles up to the mine and walk back, as the wagons will then be full of ore and all the mules can haul. All of us are dressed in prison-issue canvas coats, canvas trousers, pullover muslin shirts, and leather brogans that fit poorly.

Granite City is only another dozen miles or so beyond the mine, both nearly due west of the prison and the little berg of Deer Lodge. But that's as the crow flies, if the crow flies high. Goat Mountain will have to be edged, and even the flanks are over seven thousand feet and the top over eight.

That's the bad news, the good is my pa had a mine

and shack on the far side at just over six thousand elevation and, as it's the middle of April, the snow will likely be light there, but not getting there. The good news is no one on horseback can follow where I'll go. My pa used to call me monkey as I can climb like one—or could as it's been a while and climbing the rock walls of Deer Lodge prison is an excellent way to look down and see your liver protruding out of a .44/.40 hole in your gut.

In the valley only a few miles below Granite City is Phillipsburg, also a mining and smelter town for the many claims in the mountains adjoining, but also serving the ranchers for miles along Flint and Rock Creek and into the area they're calling the Skalkaho.

And I know folks there, in fact a lady friend, Rosy McDougle, has sent me a Christmas package every year since the lowlifes had me sent up. Rosy made the finest pasties and pies in Montana. I kept her in venison and she kept me from needing to visit Kaiser's, the town's largest saloon and bawdy house—and I wasn't a drinking man. It had been my intent to ask Rosy for her hand— even though it's said you don't need to buy the cow if you're already getting the milk. Fact is ... or was ... I loved her.

We're loaded up and Fat Freddy has just yelled "Wagon's ho," as if we're setting out to Oregon.

In three hours, I'll be ready to make my break, God willing and the creek don't rise. And I mean that literally as the flow from Goat Lake into Gold Creek has been rising as the lower snow melts with the warm days of the last week.

Some of my escape route is damn nigh straight up a rock face, and I can only hope it's ice free. I'm using that route as it's one they'd think I'm crazy to try, and one no town posse, bounty hunter, or mounted prison posse can follow.

And they're likely right. I am crazy to try.

Revenge can be a hard taskmaster and a hell of a motivator.

CHAPTER 2

THE RIDE UP HAS BEEN UNEVENTFUL—PLODDING ALONG, cussing the mules, listening to the boys in the back grousing about near everything. It ain't a bad ride with the lower slopes covered with bright yellow blooms of balsam root arrow leaf, some red paintbrush, and bluebonnets. A hawk has circled overhead, run off by a golden eagle. Meadowlarks whistle at us as we pass and a flicker gives us his raucous chatter. I'd be appreciating God's critters were I not concentrating on the task ahead.

Two of the guards will accompany eighteen of us prisoners into the mine, at least as far as the first tunnel branch, about fifty feet, where they'll plop down on their butts as the prisoners go on. They'll smoke, tell each other lies and count the mine cars coming from each branch full of ore. Two prisoners of each of the eight in each tunnel will be pushing the cars to the outside, where those two will offload the ore into the wagons. Fat Freddy will watch over me and Jasper as we tend the stock getting them to a corral and forking hay.

Then it's to the mine and drill, pick, and shovel for us as well.

Fat Freddy will stay outside and lay his fat ass down until it's time to dole out lunch for all of us—at least what's left of our lunch after he's jammed a good portion in his fat chops.

Except, this day, I'm not going into the mine at all.

The little creek snaking down the canyon runs through the corral, winding down the canyon for near three-quarters of a mile before it passes the mine. It's an easy climb following the canyon bottom upstream until it dead ends into a box canyon with damn near vertical walls. I plan to be mule-back until I reach those walls, and then it's be the monkey my pa used to call me. Up the wall. The hell of it is, should the guards reach the canyon before I top the two-hundred-foot cliff, I'll be like a target in a carnival pea shoot. So, I got to buy as much time as possible.

As the men unload, I haul a couple of buckets to the little creek, fill them and take them into the mine as far as where the shaft branches. I'm not only the mule hostler but the water boy for a short while.

Then it's Jasper's turn to haul water while I unhitch my team.

"Hurry your ass along," Fat Freddy yells, then climbs in the back of his loaded wagon and stretches out his three hundred pounds, covers his eyes with his cap and yawns. He seems to have no worries as Jasper and I have been model prisoners, 'cept for my splitting O'Toole's eyebrow and that was over four years ago. Model prisoners—up till today.

While things settle into our routine, I move quickly to

unhitch my team, lead them the fifty yards to the corral and turn them out, and trot back. The wheel mule on Fat Freddy's team, Misery he's called, is my favorite of any of the twelve. I go to work unharnessing them, but leave the headstall and reins on Misery.

I move quietly back and pull Willard's whip from its cubbyhole in the seat of his wagon. His whip has about two feet of hard handle with a nice knot of hard leather on the end so your hand doesn't slip off. Flipping it around I have a fine cudgel.

Moving back alongside the wagon, I reach in with my free hand and pat Fat Freddy on the shoulder.

"What," he says, it's obvious he's already been dozing.

He raises his head, turning slightly my way, trying to get some purchase to lift his fat self erect, but I don't wait. I whack him a good one right on the pate, and the thump echoes in the narrow canyon.

To my great surprise, he merely stares at me, his eyes swimming a mite, so I whack him another. I hate the sadistic bastard, but I don't want to add a murder to my roster of crimes—the first murder, actually, as the one I'm jailed for wasn't committed by me—and it does the job as his pig eyes roll up and he flops back, unmoving.

Fat Freddy wears a fine six-inch bladed knife as all three guards do, and carries a 73 Winchester. I grab them both and a blanket he keeps in his wagon. The weapons are a boon I hadn't expected, as I'd figured on merely jumping a mule and riding away. However, I couldn't pass up the chance to give Fat Freddy a good whack, and there the weapons lay.

Running forward, I cut Misery's reins so they're only four feet long, coil the remaining four feet, mount him bareback, and am about to give him my heels when I'm yelled at.

I spin at the voice with rifle aimed. But it's Jasper, who's running my way.

"I'm a going too," he yells.

"You only got a couple of years to go," I say.

"Not if you escape and if Fat Freddy is kilt, they gonna hang me."

"I didn't hit him that hard."

"I'm a'going," he says.

"Grab a mule. I ain't waiting."

While he runs for the corral I take the rope off my waist from under my shirt and tie a Spanish hackamore, then gig Misery up to the corral and throw him the makeshift headstall, which he puts on the biggest mule he can pick out. He swings up, leads him over and starts to close the gate behind.

"Leave it open," I command. "If they wander out, all the better." Then I give heels to Misery and we're on the gallop to the box canyon.

I give one look back before we make the first turn in the canyon, and am not pleased to see a mine car already out and a couple of prisoners standing staring after us. Then one runs back. I presume to fetch Red and O'Toole.

We're the best part of a quarter hour reaching the box canyon. I rein up, leap off Misery and drop his headstall away so he can run free.

"Bring your hackamore," I yell at Jasper and he pulls it free of his animal while I use the rein tails, make a sling for the rifle, and tie the other around my waist as my belt is only a length of twine. I need something to help secure the long knife I've taken from Fat Freddy.

Then I run for the crevice I plan to climb.

At least, at the bottom, there's brush to serve as handholds, but as it gets almost vertical the last half the way up, there's nothing but cracks in rock and the occasional narrow ledge.

"I can't do that," Jasper says, and I look back and can see the whites of his eyes all around the ebony pupils in his dark face. I can see he's truly frightened.

"You can't go back, Jasper. They'll hang you sure now."

"You didn't tell me 'bout no cliff to be climbing. Hell, I can hardly climb no ladder."

"No choice. Just follow me and do as I do. And whatever you do, don't look down."

He's dead silent, but follows as I run for the crevasse and begin to weave my way up across the esplanade of the lower portion, then attack the escarpment, which ends in vertical fissures up to jagged rocks crowning the cliffs—an edge looking like battlements on an ancient castle.

I can hear Jasper praying behind me as I reach for the first low ledge, jam a foot in a crack and hoist myself up.

"Climb, Jasper, climb," I yell, without glancing down behind me. Before I can worry too much about my companion, I'm over fifty feet high, nearly a third of the way up the steepest portion of the climb. I come upon a two-foot-wide, fairly flat ledge, get a leg up and am soon flat on my stomach on solid ground—but with another hundred feet of rock wall at my back. I damn near lose my grip as a rough-legged hawk bursts from a nest only a dozen feet away, and two chicks left behind scream a raucous call too loud for their puffy size. I quickly move aside leaving room for Jasper. He soon hoists his big body up and turns and sits, which is a mistake as he goes as pale and round-eyed as I'd guess a black man can, looking down more than the height of a tall ponderosa pine tree. He mumbles, "Sweet Jesus."

Mama hawk doesn't help as she swoops nearby, and her screams would curdle milk.

"You can say that again," I say, as I can see a wagon bouncing along in the creek bed, coming our way. The guard, Paddy O'Toole, is on the left side, and a prisoner I know only as Hack is driving. Hack is known to be a mouth who ingratiates himself to the guards by telling all he knows about what's happening in the cells. I'm surprised he's hasn't been put out of his miserable existence long ago.

"What now?" Jasper asks. We're only a hundred fifty feet up the cliff, and even from where the wagon has reined up, only a hundred yards. An easy shot for a poor marksman.

I unsling the Winchester, work the lever and check the load. I want to be ready, but have no interest in killing a guard—even one who's as worthless a human being as O'Toole has proven himself to be. He dismounts, carrying his Winchester, while looking up at our precarious perch. I can hear him laughing. He moves to the rear of the wagon, and I can see him laying the rifle up on the tailgate to steady his aim.

So, I lay down the sights on the back of the wagon and quickly put a shot through the tailgate, about gut high on O'Toole. Splinters fly, O'Toole throws up his arms, and the Winchester flies away. He goes to his back, but wiggling and frothing around.

"Well, you done done it now," Jasper says.

"Him or us, pardner. With luck he ain't dead, just nicked and full of splinters. I didn't hold dead center."

Hack jumps from the wagon and runs around to O'Toole, then turns and yells up at us. "Let me load him?"

"Load him and get the hell out of here," I yell back, and he does.

"Ain't no going back now," Jasper says. "They'll hang me sure just to watch me dance."

"Didn't plan on going back no how," I say and stand and re-sling the rifle. "So, pardner, let's get up this wall before Red shows up, and we're flat on the wall and can't shoot back."

"Climb," Jasper says, and I do.

CHAPTER 3

ROCK CLIMBING IS BUSINESS FOR A SPIDER, NOT A HEAVY porker like Jasper. And I only say porker as he's thick as one. Where I'm a couple of inches short of six feet and one hundred seventy pounds, Jasper is all of six feet and more, and I'd guess over two hundred seventy. He's mostly muscle, but has a protrusion some would mistake for a fat belly and thighs damn near as big as my waist. A fella built like that has trouble staying away from the rock wall so's he can see his handholds and anticipate his next move. I truly fear he won't make the top and am continually encouraging—I hope inspiring—him as I place hand after hand and floppy brogan foot toeing as deep as I can drive them into cracks. Occasionally I have a vertical crack and yell at him to show him how to jam a hand in when you can't get a finger hold.

It should be getting warmer as the day progresses, but damn if it ain't getting colder, and the breeze has picked up. A wind is not to my liking. A real wind could be the death of us.

When we only have twenty-five feet to go, if I'm not

looking at a false top, Jasper flattens against the wall and calls out to me, "Jack, I'm done. I can't make it."

I pause, and against my own good advice look down and see him flat as a slug, even his cheek pressing against the cold stone.

"Jasper, we only got about four of you to go. It's a damn sight shorter to reach the top than the bottom. It looks to me like there's a rain working up and wet ain't our friend. You take a little blow and we're gonna top this wall and head for a warm spot I know."

"Warm spot. He'll, I'm sweating like Blackfeet Indians was holding my feet to the fire now."

"And if you'll look just ahead of me and to the right, you see that crevasse, it's got lots of growth and hand-holds. Hang on for just a bit more."

I hear him sigh deeply and encourage him again. "Jasper, I'll bet you a dime against a donut hole I'll have a fat deer down by supper time. How long has it been since you had a thick steak?"

"Six years or more."

"Then it's only six hours to another. Now, push off that wall, don't look down and climb."

"Damn if you ain't a bossy bastard."

"My ma and pa was married. Now climb!"

And he does, and I'm happy to say the edge I was studying was truly the top. I give him a hand and pull him the last couple of feet as he throws a leg over the edge. We both go to our backs, but I quickly raise up, hearing the clatter of iron-shod hooves on rocks, and peer over the edge to see Red, the third guard, studying the walls.

He's late to find an easy target.

There's a thick fir forest behind us, and I don't make a move until he's looking away, then lay back down.

I elbow Jasper. "Ol' Red is down there, lamenting the fact he don't have a couple of escapees plastered on the rock wall."

"I don' know what lamenting be, but I'm glad we ain't still there."

"I'll bet you know what a warm fireplace is, and will be happy to know there's one about a mile or two from where we're dawdling. That is if some freeloader ain't warming his sef' at the cabin my pa built near a worthless hole he thought would be a bonanza. Let's go."

"How about that steak?" he asks as he pushes away from the edge before getting to his feet.

"God willing we'll see us a fat doe on the way. Let's go.

But it's not a doe we see, it's an elk. And he's not used to seeing folks as he's obliges me by standing and staring at us—and dropping in his tracks with a well-placed heart shot. Of course, at sixty yards it was nothing to brag about.

Still, I'm glad I haven't lost my touch with a Winchester.

Two can't easily tote a full-grown elk, as it's near three hundred pounds. Even though at this elevation it's near freezing and will be well below tonight, Jasper removes his coat and ties it around heart, liver and back straps. He hangs it around his neck as a back pack and slings both hindquarters over his shoulders. I have the forequarters on mine, and we're off.

Pa's claim and cabin are easy to find as there's a series of rock spires just above it leading nearly to the top of

Goat Mountain. But I was right, it's no more than a mile of easy hike around the mountain.

But as I worried, there's smoke coming from the stone chimney.

I position Jasper fifty yards from the cabin door, south facing on the south slope of the mountain. "I'm going on up there with a forequarter to bargain with. Probably best if'n it's a white face looking for shelter. If there's trouble, you got the Winchester."

"Probably best, but don't be leaving me out in the cold."

"Wouldn't think of it. Besides, you've got the best of the elk."

He gives me a crooked smile, then waves me on. "Get on with it. My mouth's waterin'."

I give him a smile and a nod and am off. As I near, I shout out. "Hello, the cabin!"

I hold short twenty feet from the door, and yell again. "Hello, the cabin! I got a haunch of elk here needs cooking, and I'll trade for some shelter."

I hear a bar being removed and the door opens but only a couple of inches and it's so dark inside I can't make out the occupant.

I'm surprised to hear a female voice. "What you want, stranger?"

"How about a place for me and my friend to hole up for the night? We'll provide supper and leave you with a fresh hindquarter—maybe more."

"I been over the mountain to Deer Lodge. Them look like prison duds to me."

"Yes, ma'am. We were just released and are on our way to Granite looking for work."

"You got the makings for a fire?"

"I got steel and flint."

She opens the door a little more and I'm surprised to see I should have sent Jasper. She's a pretty cocoa brown with skin smooth as a trout.

That's the best of it. She has a double barrel shotgun in hand. But she smiles. "Y'all go up to the edge of the forest and make yourself a fire to keep warm. When my man gets outta the mine, he'll come fetch you if'n he's a mind to."

"Yes'um. You close and bar that door and I'll leave this forequarter on the stoop. Appreciate y'all considering the shelter for us."

"Gotta do things like Jesus laid out."

"Yes, ma'am. My friend is a man of color, but I don't imagine you'd mind that?"

"Don't look like it, do it?" she says, and flashes white teeth at me, then closes the door and I hear the bar going back in place. I move forward and lean the forequarter on the door. Then yell, "We'll be up under that first big fir tree."

But she doesn't answer. Before I join back up with Jasper, I hear the door open and turn back to see her pulling the forequarter inside.

We have a nice fire roaring as there's plenty of downfall in the forest behind us without stealing a log from one of the half dozen stacks scattered about. It seems the mister of the house has plenty left over from winter. I hold us over with a couple of shards of jerky each, until off to our left at the mouth of the mine, a voice rings out, "What the hell are y'all doing burning my wood?"

CHAPTER 4

He's forty yards from us, but isn't bashful about sounding out.

"We fetched these logs out of the woods," Jasper yells back. "We got meat," he says, pointing to the three remaining hindquarters hanging over a fir limb, then at his coat still rolled up with back-straps, heart and liver.

We can hear the tall thin black man "Humph," even at this distance. He strides our way, a pick over his shoulder, a shovel in the other hand. When he's twenty yards short of us, he stops suddenly. "Y'all escaped convicts from over the mountain? Them is prison duds."

His hair and beard are white as the snow on up the mountain, and he's as tall as Jasper, but half the weight. In fact, he looks all bone and sinew.

I speak before Jasper can answer. I've found him to be too honest at times.

"Yes, sir, we're from there, but just released yesterday. Headed for Granite City to find work."

"They didn't have the clothes you wore when they checked you in?"

"Hell, that warden would sell our teeth and finger-nails would they fall off. We had to give up the coin we came with to buy these canvas duds."

He gives another "humph," then asks. "What y'all want here? We barely got enough for our own selves."

This time Jasper answers before I can. "All we want is a roof for the night. We brought your woman a fore-quarter—elk haunch—and will leave you with another hindquarter should you oblige us."

He stands and surveys us up and down, then, drops the shovel, steps forward and extends a hand to Jasper. "Henry Sutterville. Woman be Maggy Jane."

Jasper shakes with him and offers, "We mean y'all no harm, Mr. Sutterville. We'll be on our way, first light."

"Henry will do, and you are?"

"Jeff ... Jeff Smith," Jasper lies, then nods at me, "And that's my pardner, George."

The tall thin miner offers me a paw, one with a quarter inch of hard callus, well-earned I'd wager from that pick and shovel.

"Y'all got a last name, George?"

We'd crossed one creek I knew on the way here, Dead Horse, and it was all I could think of offhand. "Horse-man," I come with and have no idea why.

"Funny name. You an Indian?" he asks.

I have to laugh at that. I got the black hair but never saw a savage with blue eyes. "No, sir. It's an Irish name. Proud old Irish name."

"Humph," he says again, then adds, "They's a trough out back of the cabin at the corral, and a barn where y'all can fight shy of the weather. You can wash up there.

Maggy Jane don't allow no dirty hands at her table. I hope that blood on your trousers come from that elk?"

"Yes, sir," Jasper says, and laughs. "I guess we coulda found a water hole and scrubbed down, but it was a mite cold to try and dry our duds."

"Well, sir," Henry replies, "get to the trough a'fore it freezes over."

It's cold at this elevation, but when you glance up and see a skein of ducks or geese heading north, you know Spring is here.

In addition to cutting up the forequarter and making a stew that filled a four-quart Dutch oven with meat, potatoes, onions and carrots, Mrs. Sutterville has made drop biscuits that threaten to float off the plate. Smothered in fresh churned butter and honey, it's all Jasper and I can do to stop reaching for more. At the end of the meal, Henry does us the honor of sharing a smoke and a pull on a jug of corn liquor he's distilled himself. He's a man of many trades and talents

Maggy Jane Sutterville is not only a fine cook but a comely woman as well, with a complexion as smooth as the butter she's churned, and lithe and light-footed as a doe antelope. Jasper seems shy as a ten-year-old, keeping his eyes down so as not to insult her or her man by staring. I believe he's smitten and conclude it's a good thing we leave with first light.

As we relax, each with a corncob pipe fashioned by Henry, I try and assure our early departure. "Henry, we'll be leaving with first light and won't bother your lady for breakfast. I don't imagine you have a little jerky to trade for the rest of our elk?"

"I do, but it don't seem a fair trade. I'll throw in a pound of hardtack. You got cartridges for that .44/.40?"

"Just what's in the tube."

He looks us both over before he adds. "I guess the warden throwed in that Winchester and them huntin' knives with that little bit of coin you had to pay for your duds?"

"I guess not," I say honestly. "But they got plenty down at Deer Lodge and likely won't miss this one much."

He nods, and says, "For a while there I was thinking you was the kind of fella who'd piss down my neck and tell me it was a'raining."

He gives me a grin, then leans back and gives the corncob a couple of puffs. "I damn near died in Andersonville. One of the few Negras imprisoned there. Most was shot down like dogs just for being men of color fightin' for the north. Don't have to tell you I wasn't treated so good by them devil guards. Had I not been captured so near the end of the war, I would have sure died. Them white boys that was my fellow prisoners shared food with me as I was handy with diggin' holes and we had us a long tunnel working. We was a few feet outside the fence and only a week from making a break when General Grant met up with Lee and the war was done ended. You think I'm close to the bone now, you shoulda seen me back in '65', a heavy breeze woulda blowed me over. Thing is, I got no liking for prisons and less for prison guards. I wouldn't piss on a prison guard or most any law dog were he dying of thirst. So y'all see, I don't give a tinker's damn if you fellas is running from the prison law."

Jasper speaks up, "Henry, is there anything we can for you before we light out?"

"Fact is I got a half dozen timbers shaped for shoring, but have a hell of a time lifting and shoring up at the same time. If y'all could give me a couple of hours come morning I'd be obliged, and Maggy Jane would fix you a larrupin' fine breakfast then lunch to send you off."

Jasper and I both nod. "Fact is," I say, "I don't want to wander around Granite or Phillipsburg in the daylight and we're only a half day there. Right?"

"Yep," Henry nods knowingly. "You know they got the wire there now, leastways as far as Phillipsburg and, last I heard, they was coming up the mountain with it. They'll be on the lookout for y'all. Negra man and a blue-eyed Irishman travelling together. You'll stand out like a wart on the preacher's nose. I got a couple of work shirts and I'm gonna trade you for them prison duds so y'all won't be quite so obvious. While y'all are giving me a hand, Maggy Jane will sew a panel in the back of one so's it fits Jeff. Won't be pretty, but he'll be able to button it shut."

"Then we'll go down the mountain after lunch," I offer.

He adds, "Should it come to you getting' reamed by the law dogs, tell them y'all saw them shirts on the line and traded them you own self, so I ain't the one getting the reamin'."

We both give him a "yes, sir" at the same time, then smile and nod.

I have not mentioned to Mr. Sutterville that he's likely occupying my cabin and working my mine. However, I have no idea if my ma sold it after pa passed and before she did. If not, I'm the only heir. I'll cross that bridge when I've solved my other problems—and likely putting the Harringtons, Sheriff Papadopoulos, Deputy Morgan Tuttle, and Cornelius Caphorn in the ground will certainly leave me behind bars or kicking at the end of a rope—so the Suttervilles might as well continue as is and there's no sense bothering them with minor legalities.

The last few miles to Granite, mostly down the mountain, is an easy hike and we arrive on a bluff with the busy little mining town a couple of hundred yards below. We've skirted two busy mines on the way down but remained unseen.

We're watching the town fill with miners as the sun drops below the mountain top, streaking the sky with red and gold. Both of us spread out belly down on a rock watching the town awaken with miners and teamsters and merchants just off work, when we both jump with a challenge from our rear.

"What hell you two up to?"

CHAPTER 5

WE BOTH SPIN TO OUR BACKS, ME WITH THE RIFLE IN HAND and Jasper with his big paw on the hilt of his knife, but the voice belongs to an old Chinese lady.

Jasper answers, "We takin' a rest is all. What the hell are you up to?"

"I herb lady. Mushroom, herb, lots coming soon."

"You live in Granite?" I ask.

She laughs, showing only every other missing tooth in her head. "You think I live in cave?"

"No, ma'am. You know the sheriff in Granite?"

"Sure, Mr. Max good man. I do shirts."

"Max?" I ask.

"Yes. Mr. Max."

"Where's Papadopoulos?"

"Mr. Tony. He die. Bank robber shoot in belly."

"Too bad," I say through gritted teeth.

"Too bad?" Jasper asks.

"Yeah, I was saving him for me," I say, a little sadly, "and the good Lord and some damn robber cheated me out of that lying sheriff," and turn back to the Chinee lady.

"And Tuttle?"

"Mr. Morgan now town marshal down in P-burg."

"And Harrington and his brat?"

"He have son. All move P-burg. Harrington own Kaiser demon water and whores."

"How about Cornelius Caphorn?"

"Mr. Corney? He run Hard Rock. He good man. He help me lots times."

That makes me grimace a little as I damn sure don't agree. "What's your name, ma'am?"

"Ling Su, white devils call me Weed Woman."

That makes my grimace turn to grin. "Well, Weed Woman, when our shirts need a launder and a press we'll be looking you up."

"Okie dokie. Ten cents. Clean, no wrinkle."

As she walks away studying the ground, I note her braided gray queue hangs to her butt.

I plop down on a rock beside Jasper. "We've got to move in case she says something to someone."

"Phillipsburg?" he asks.

"You can go if you want to. I have business here."

"Hell, Jack, in for a penny, in for a pound. Sounds like all them fellas need to give the Devil his due."

"Well, sir, I plan to arrange the introduction."

We move away a couple of hundred yards into a thick tangle of chokecherry but still with a view of the town and watch agile bats snagging insects for a while, then when it's dead dark with only a half-waning moon we stand and work our way out of the tangle. As we enter the little two-dozen-building town between what turns out to be the tonsorial parlor and the assay office, I can't help but note that both are boarded up. It seems Granite is shutting down. No wonder the Harringtons and Deputy Tuttle have moved their thieving operations to Phillipsburg. As we near Broadway Street—the only street in Granite—there's a drunk either asleep or passed out, near the end of the alley leaning against the building. He has a floppy brimmed hat. Not wanting to be recognized, I relieve him of his chapeau. Had I two bits, I'd leave it in exchange and that would likely be overpaying.

Then I think I recognize and remember him. Norval Hettinger, whose daddy is, or was, the town banker. And who was on the jury that sent me up. I thought him somewhat a simpleton, and his current state gives me no reason to doubt my former assessment. I consider just cutting his throat as he's too stupid to share this earth will decent folk, but I don't fancy having an imbecile's death on my conscience.

He has a poke tucked in his belt, a little leather bag that I find is filled with over one hundred twenty dollars in gold coin. As I'm sure someone will relieve him of his riches before the night is over, I break the law for the second time in my life—breaking prison being the first—and relieve him of two twenty-dollar gold coins and a fine Navy Colt sidearm. I feel a little guilty but no so much as to not have a stake and a sidearm.

I hand the Colt and a coin to Jasper, who acts like he doesn't want to take it. "Don't worry about it," I reassure him, "I know this lout as he was on the jury what sent me up. He owes me."

Jasper nods, pockets the coin and shoves the Colt into his rope belt. "Sounds right then," he says.

It's dead dark; however, there are still two or three
dozen fellas wandering the street. Music and light pours
from Hard Rock Harry's. The town's three coal oil street-
lights are circled by a hundred moths each.

When I last saw Cornelius Caphorn, I was seven years
younger with no beard. Now I hope my two inches of face
whiskers and unruly hair to my shoulders is enough to
hide my identity.

The bat wing doors seem the only way in, so I take it.
Negras are not always welcome in a saloon, so Jasper
and I agree he should wait outside and across the street
near a couple of decent looking riding horses, should we
need a rapid exit. Besides, this part of the world may
likely be on the prod for a black and white running
together.

It's a fine-looking saloon, even nicer than I remember.
A scantily clad lady with generous attributes decorates
the backbar, smiling from a painting at least six feet long,
nearly a life-size image. Three faro tables, a poker table, a
wheel of chance, and a table with a game I don't recognize are each nearly full of players. A wheel of chance is
tended by a fine-looking pleasure lady if you enjoy those
pleasingly plump. Two of the faro tables are dealt by
women, but the third and unknown game are dealt
by men.

The place is smoky, hanging down near head height,
as most the customers are sucking cigars or pipes. Those
not smoking are chomping chaw and spittoons oblige
them every six feet along the walls, beneath the tables,
and along the brass rail at the foot of the bar. A fairly
clean towel hangs from a hook every six feet along the
bar. A hogshead barrel dead center in the room is filled

with goober peanuts and the floor is littered with shells, atop a scattering of sawdust.

Half the three dozen men in the place are heeled, but most with sidearms. A couple, like me, have long arms at hand.

The bartender is a bull of a man, the devil's horns being wisps of side hair below a shiny baldness that's his pate. His eyes are continually sweeping the place. Even as he draws a beer or pours three fingers of whiskey. As the subject of my wrath is nowhere to be seen, I decide to learn something and go to the table with the game I haven't seen. I stand behind a couple of miners who have a fair stack of nickel, dime, two and four bit, and a few dollar chips at hand.

As the dealer shuffles to deal again, I ask them, "What's this game?"

The one I've noticed is the most talkative of the two, turns and eyes me. "You look like you ain't seen a dollar since the war. However, the game is vingt-et-un, a game the frogs brought from France to torture us with."

"How's that again?" I ask.

"Vingt-et-un is what they call it. Some call it twenty-one or lately called Blackjack. Object is to get twenty-one by the count, or at least beat the dealer. You go over twenty-one, you bust and the dealer wins, even if he busts after you do. You bet whatever you want ahead of the deal."

"Can the dealer bust?"

"You bet he can, but he has to stand on seventeen and hit—take another card—on sixteen. A face or ten and an ace is called a blackjack. If the dealer blackjacks it's over, unless you do too, then it's called a push—a tie—and nobody wins. In fact, any tie is a push. Nobody wins or loses."

"Looks pretty simple to me," I say.

"Don't they all?" he replies with a snicker, then returns as the dealer starts again.

I watch for a quarter hour until the talkative fella loses all his chips and leaves, and then I take his seat and buy five dollars' worth of chips. I've always been a fair hand at math, and have an excellent memory. There are only fifty-two cards in a deck; sixteen of those count ten, and four aces that count either one or eleven. So, I figure right away that if you know what's left in the deck you know the odds of what you might get if you hit. I can see that the dealer shows one of his two cards on the deal. That tells me if he has a five or six up he's more likely to bust so it might be wise for a player to stand on anything when hitting might result in his busting first.

In a half hour, I've got over twenty-five dollars in chips and I'd like to keep playing, but Mr. Cornelius 'Corny' Caphorn has wandered in the rear of the place and taken a stool at the end of the bar.

Unfortunately, he's plopped up next to a one-eyed beanpole with red hair who looks like he's wandered through a tornado. And he's obviously sitting shotgun in Hard Rock Harry's, as a double barrel is close at hand. He would be the fella who settles all disputes

I guess it's time to say howdy, and goodbye, to Mr. Caphorn, no matter if he's guarded by a side-by-side twelve-gauge man killer.

Still, it's time for Corny to say howdy to Beelzebub.

CHAPTER 6

LOOKING OVER THE PLACE BEFORE ENTERING I'D DECIDED there is no rear entrance. That turns out not to be exactly accurate. A sign near a rear door has an arrow pointing out back and the word privy. So, I wander that way, interested to note that Corny and the shotgun guard pay no attention as I pass behind them. It not only interests me, but it also sends a wave of heat up my backbone to the point I want to give Red, the shotgun guard, a rap on the head bone. Then spend a few minutes with the Winchester shoved so far into Corny's ribs he can taste the steel before he feels the fire and lead. But I maintain and pass quietly.

The rear yard is enclosed by an eight-foot vertical plank fence, with no gate or windows. Before going back inside I give the rough planks a push and decide a good kick would fold them. Folding two will provide passage for a man half again my girth.

With Corny so confident he pays no attention to those passing behind, it will be a simple matter to shove the Winchester into his ribs and blow him to hell, but that would offer me little satisfaction. I spent seven years dreaming of how I'd get even with the four lowlifes who gave false testimony to put me away in order to save Horace Harrington from the hangman. I had only been saved from hanging because of conflicting testimony, mostly the fact the Baptist preacher testified he'd seen me on the other end of town the same instant a scream was heard over most of Granite. That, and the fact Harrington knew I was being railroaded and didn't insist on my hanging. I guess he had a tinge of conscience.

Sorta hoping he'll recognize me and give me reason to unload on him, I climb up on the stool next to him. He barely glances over.

The barrel-big bartender comes my way, wiping the bar around mugs and shot glasses as he does.

He stops across the bar, placing ham-size hands on the far edge and leaning my way, he asks, "You just decorating the place, Blackjack, or are you spending some of that coin you won."

"Blackjack?" I ask.

"Yep, that's what the boys hung on you. They said you was one lucky owlhoot."

"I guess good at cards don't count?"

"One day it does, next maybe not. You spendin', or just decoratin' the place?"

"I'll have three fingers of Old Fitzgerald with a beer back." He starts away but I stop him. "And bring my two friends here another."

He nods and moves away, and that gets Corny's attention. He turns my way and eyes me carefully. I wonder if he's recognized me. But he sticks out a paw and we shake.

"It ain't often a customer buys the boss a drink," he says, with a wide grin.

"My pleasure," I say, but it almost chokes me.

He eyes me again, then asks, "You ain't a miner or a drover. What brings you to Granite?"

I give him a crooked grin. "Got a debt to settle."

"Fella ought to settle what he owes. You owe someone here in town?"

It's time to change the subject, so I do. "Old chum of mine. This is your joint?"

"It is, and it ain't a joint. We run a fair place. We don't water the whiskey. We deal a fair game. We support the local church and the miners' widows' and orphans' fund."

I suddenly realize I didn't notice any telegraph wires coming into town, not that I necessarily would have. But I ask, "I need to telegraph my folks over in Helena. Where's the key?"

"We've been trying to get them to run it up the mountain, but the nearest operator is down at Phillipsburg. Speaking of that, don't I know you from somewhere, maybe P-Burg?"

It seems he's beginning to get the feeling he knows me, but he likely has no idea I've just given the slip to Deer Lodge. I guess it's time to fish or cut bait, so I say, "Enjoy your drink." I stand and act as if I'm moving away. Instead I jam the barrel of my Winchester into Red's ribs, and reach across him for the shotgun. His jaw drops, but he makes no aggressive moves. I tuck the shotgun under my arm and with my other hand I grab Corny's Colt out of his holster.

"What the ...."

"Corny," I ask, "do you remember lying through your

teeth to Judge Mort Allenthorp about seeing me run out of the Palace Hotel some seven years ago."

"You're Jack Brannigan," he says, turning a little white.

"I knew that," I say, then add, "but I hear I'm now called Blackjack which suits me fine as I have black-hearted work to do. I'm offended you don't recognize a face that should have haunted you these past seven years, but I guess you've tried to put me out of your black heart."

"You're in prison," he exclaims, his jaw slack.

"You got bad eyesight or what?" I ask.

"I guess it must be fading as I let you slip up on me."

"Slip up, hell. I plopped it right down beside your dumb ass."

The bartender arrives across from us again, and snaps, "What the hell is going on here?"

I have the shotgun in one hand shoved into Corny's back and the Winchester still in Red's ribs, I shift the shotgun a foot and it's now centered on the bartender's wide frame.

So, speaking clearly so I'm understood, I instruct him, "Friend, I've got no interest in spilling your guts, so you move on down to the other end of the bar and stand quiet. With luck you're in Corny's will. If Red don't make a sudden move, you or he are likely the new owner of Harry's."

"You won't get out of here, Brannigan," Corny says.

"You think not, Corny? It don't matter much to me, so long as your guts are all over that backbar."

"You know Harrington had my wife and kids holed up somewhere, turned out in that mine of his, threatening me, and I had no choice."

I don't normally curse, but I feel the need. "Bullshit."

"You and I are gonna walk out of here and down to my place. My wife is likely just finishing feeding my six kids, which you seem willing to make orphans out of, and I won't say a word. She don't know you from Adam's off ox. You ask her why I had to lie at that trial and she'll tell you."

"Bullshit," I say.

"No bull. You can shoot me dead, but I had no choice." Then he turns to his shotgun guard and speaks loud enough the bartender can hear, "I don't want anybody killed, so you two stand at ease. We're taking a walk and don't need company."

He gets a nod from both of them.

"Damn you." I look around and note that none of the three dozen men nor the three women dealers are paying a bit of attention to us. I jab the Winchester deeper into Red's ribs. Then I give him instructions. "You show your face outside this saloon and I shoot the boss through his backbone. You understand?"

CHAPTER 7

RED, THE SHOTGUN GUARD, NODS, AND I BACK AWAY AND
let both muzzles drop just enough to not look threatening to the customers. "Move it," I say, not wanting to kill
a man who was only trying to protect his family. Now I'm
conflicted.

As we pass the big bartender Corny extends a hand,
palm out, telling him to lay off. He stands quietly as we
push through the batwings.

But I have a very sour taste in my mouth as I follow
Corny down Broadway Street, glancing back over my
shoulder with every third step to make sure the bartender
or shotgun guard are not following. We stride quickly for
two blocks near level, then a block downhill to a nice
whitewashed house with a picket fence. From the light
pouring from the windows through lace curtains I can
see the stepping stones leading to the door are lined with
rose bushes, already budding with yellow and red
blooms.

He leads the way in.

"Martha," he yells as we enter the house, where a

fistful of youngsters from knee to chest high are gathered in front of a stone fireplace, each with a book or tablet at hand. They all jump to their feet as we enter. And almost in unison say, "Good evening, pa."

It's probably the nicest thing I've seen in seven years.

"Back to your studies," Corny instructs and I follow him on into the kitchen, where another fire glows in a handsome nickel and black iron Star Range, covered with pots.

"Martha, this is my friend, Jack."

She moves over and bows slightly and smiles. "Do I need to set another place?"

"Jack?" Corny asks, as if I'm invited.

"Sorry, Corny, but I can't stay." I glance at the wall over a small table and see an embroidered sampler, "Bless this House." My ma had one much the same.

His missus asks, "Can I set your firearm on the rack."

"Won't be stayin', ma'am."

He turns again to his wife, "Jack has heard some rumors about that son of a ...."

"Corny, the children ...."

"Sorry. About Harrington and why I had to lie at that trial."

She eyes me a little closer, then starts to ask, "You ... your ...." But decides against it and turns back to Corny. "You sure you want me to talk about that?"

"Dead sure," he says, and I understand his statement far better than does she.

She almost immediately starts shedding tears, and can barely speak. I'm convinced and put my arm around her shoulders at the risk of being offensive, telling her how sorry I am to have asked. She sputters plenty but gets the sordid tale out. I'm really not a dang bit sorry she does as I'm convinced. It's kept me from shooting down a man with six nice kids who seems to have a fine wife.

I turn to Corny and give him a tight smile. "Glad I came to meet your family. Would you mind walking me out. I turn to his wife, "Thank you, ma'am for the invitation. Another time, I hope." He does walk with me and, as soon as we exit, I spot Red, the shotgun guard, now with Winchester in hand and he's on one knee at the gate. Luckily, I've followed Corny out and he's between us. Corny yells out, "Rufus, it's all a misunderstanding. Jack and I are good friends again. Head on back to work."

What neither Rufus nor Corny realize is that Jasper is at an alley entrance only fifty feet beyond Rufus.

Red, who I now know as Rufus, rises slowly, and yells out, "You sure, boss?"

"Sure as you're a brindle top. Go on now while I bid Jack goodbye."

He moves away, but watches me for the first fifty feet of his retreat.

"Jack," Corny says, and seems sincere, "I can't tell you how sorry I am. Harrington is a low life son-of-a-bitch and he wouldn't have hesitated drowning my kids in a horse trough had I not done as he commanded. I told him I wouldn't lie, and the next I knew …. He owns the majority of Hard Rock Harry's. To say he had me by the shorthairs is no exaggeration."

I sigh deeply before responding. "I ain't got no kids nor any kin, so I won't try and judge you for trying to save your'n. The good Lord will do that when the time comes. I can't say as I forgive you. I figure you owe me something."

He shrugs. "Guess I do. What can I do to make it right?"

"We need horses and gear and a spare set of duds."

"We?"

"I got a pardner who had a muzzle laid down on that Rufus fella. He mighta shot me, but old brindle top would now be cold meat, and likely you too, had he done so."

"Hmmm," Corny says, but doesn't argue. Then he adds, "Waterson owns the mercantile, and Hilty's the hostler here in town. Both of them are in my saloon, and both of them owe me. Let's go fetch 'em up."

Inside an hour Jasper and I both have a set of new store-bought duds. Including fine tan colored beaver hats. I wear a new cartridge belt full of .44/40's and have a shiny new seven-dollar Navy Colt riding at my side. We each have two boxes of cartridges in our saddlebags, drover's saddles with martingales and billet straps for steep riding, and with roping horns and lariats hanging aside. Waterson couldn't fit Jasper's big feet with riding boots, but fits him with brogans. I wear a fine pair of leather calf-highs. Both of us now sport ankle-length sheepskin-lined dusters that will not only serve as warmth, but as bed rolls. And they each have deep pockets inside and out. Their dark tan coloring will blend in with the fall colors should we need to hide out in forest or field. We are nearly two hundred dollars into Corny's purse by the time we ride out.

My buckskin gelding, Sand, seems fine to me; quick to rein and backs up like a cougar was facing him. And Jasper sits a half-Percheron, half-Morgan seventeen-hand gray gelding, Apollo, which didn't even stumble or moan when the big man mounted.

I've satisfied about two of those I hunt and haven't fired a shot. One dead by the hand of a bandit, gut shot and died hard, which was what I wished for him. The other, I'm resigned to forgive, as having no kin, I seem to particularly value the kin of those folks I know, even if those I know are someone I likely should hate. It's said blood is thicker than water. I believe it, and wish I had kin so I could get the feel of it.

Colonel Maxmillian Harrington is the head of the snake and his fangs have proven to be sharp. His son, my old friend, Horace Harrington, was someone I looked up to for the three years we were supposedly good buddies. Morgan Tuttle is now the City Marshal of Phillipsburg; a man I never liked nor admired and a man who proved himself a lying scumbag. All now residents of the little mining and cattle town of Phillipsburg.

They won't be hard to find.

CHAPTER 8

WE DECIDE TO RIDE AT LEAST HALFWAY TO PHILLIPSBURG IN the moonlight and to find a place to lay up off the two-track wagon road under a thick fir tree in a bed of needles. It's only three miles to P-Burg as the crow flies, and I remember a small creek about halfway there so we plod along for what I judge to be a half hour, then turn uphill until we find a small clearing. We tie the horses to a couple of small lodgepole pines and, after gnawing some jerky, curl up in our new dusters, cozy as a toad in a mudhole. It's a fine nest in soft beds of decomposing needles with their dusky smell, a cold creek nearby, meadow larks singing and Clark's nutcrackers sassing.

We awake before the sun crests the mountains to the east and are proudly saddled and cantering the last mile and half to Phillipsburg. We rein up a couple of hundred yards shy of the first buildings to let the dust settle, then ride to the top of a small hill that overlooks the town of a hundred or so buildings. A half dozen on the main street, Broadway Street, are substantial—brick or stone construction—including the bank, a hotel, a saddlery and harness shop, an assay office, and a two or more saloons including the Kaiser, a large saloon, restaurant, and inn with rooms on the second floor and cribs out back for use of the soiled doves. The building is at least fifty feet fronting on Broadway and over one hundred feet deep but fronting on a side street, North Montgomery. There's a City Hall and four-cell jail and sheriff's office in its own nearby building, but they are three or four blocks to the northwest of Broadway. The main business in town is an ore smelter, Deidesheimer's, so smoke is a constant companion, as is noise from the crusher. It's been at work all night so the grinding of ore is unrelenting. It operates twenty-four hours a day. Smoke roils from its stacks, and the crunch of rock niggles the ears and irritates like the constant buzz of a wasp circling for attack.

The rest of the town is just waking, with only a few merchants opening clanging metal shutters and clattering goods and signs onto the boardwalks so they can be seen.

We watch for a few minutes but are both ravishingly hungry and in need of a cup of hot coffee. It's not cold, in the forties I'd guess, and warming to near sixty in the day. Before we take on the town, I suggest to Jasper, "You go in first. That sign on Kaiser's says saloon and restaurant, so I know we can get steak and eggs there, but it might be wise to split up. You go to Kaiser's as they don't know your ugly mug. I'll look for another grease pot. Remember, they got the wire here, so they'll be on the lookout for a colored man and an ugly Irish lout travelling together. So, if we pass on the street, act like I got the epizootic."

"What the hell is the epizootic?" he asks, and I laugh.

"Never thought on it. Act like I got the measles, how's that."

"I been jawing with you plenty. I'll enjoy the lack of it."

"Ha ha. You're as funny as one of those cold stone cells over the mountain. See you back at our camp spot come supper time and we'll reconnoiter over a shot of good whiskey."

"I guess. Reconnoiter don't hurt do it?"

I laugh, and explain, "Meet up and make a plan."

"It's springtime. I wonder if that Kaiser's has mountain oysters. I been dreaming of fried mountain oysters or maybe lamb fries."

"Go. It's too soon for them to have posters on us. Try and look small and prosperous."

"Never been prosperous, but I'll buy me a fifty-cent cigar, will that do?"

"Go."

He laughs and gigs the big gray away.

It's my plan to search out my old love, Rosy McDougle, and I'm praying she hasn't married up with some lowlife hooligan—not that she would. Likely she's hooked up the town doctor or mayor or some highfalutin type.

I wait until I know Jasper is well into town, probably already with steak and eggs or mountain oysters and eggs in front of him, and give Sand my heels. I ride Broadway from east to west and back again and don't see a bake shop. The town is shaking loose its kinks, and drays and farm wagons are already being dodged by horsebackers and fellas on shank's mare sloshing around puddles and bogs in the road.

But I soon see Queeny's Grub and Grog, tie Sand up in front and go in. You can usually judge a café by the number of customers, and had a grubby miner not gotten up from the counter, I wouldn't have gotten a seat without waiting. It's been seven years since I had a menu in front of me, and I spend a long time enjoying the thought of a choice. The man behind the counter comes my way three times before I finally order oatmeal, then fried eggs and pork chops and a side of fried potatoes. The coffee comes in mugs as big as both my fists and I can barely finish a cup while it's still hot, even though it's tongue-scalding when poured.

It's a feast fit for a king and I'm glad I'm three quarters through it before I glance over my shoulder and see my old friend Horace Harrington, still boyish with too many teeth showing when he smiles. He's across a small table from City Marshal Morgan Tuttle. I don't know if I'm lucky or doomed, but the fact is, they are so busy haranguing a chubby waitress that I'm the last thing they notice. Like with Corny, I have the urge to finish my meal and just wander over and shove the muzzle of my new Colt to the nape of Tuttle's neck and blowing a mess over Horace's steak and eggs before I put one in his own brisket. But that would be anticlimactic when there's only three left to settle with. So, I decide to finish my breakfast, let them leave and follow Horace as I have no idea where he hangs his hat.

Tuttle, I'm sure, has an office, likely in the City Hall up the hill.

I want to get the lay of the land, and the lair of my enemies. To be truthful, I want to at least pay my respects to Rosy McDougle before I have to kick up rocks beating hoofs out of town. I owe her for being the only one to pay me any attention while I was in that hellhole, Deer Lodge.

I drop a half dollar on the bar—forty cents plus a generous tip—and follow Horace out. He and Tuttle shake hands, and I'm wondering which one is leaving for an extended trip, as I overhear, "I'll see you upon return," and I'm worried. Maybe I should just blow them both all to hell right here on the street. But I grit my teeth and chide myself, knowing there will be a better time and place. I choose to follow Horace as they separate, but not too closely. He's had time to make a quarter block. I start after him, but after only a few steps, I'm face to face with a large woman in a bustled dress, and jerk the hat off my head.

"Ma'am, I'm in need of a cake for a special event. Can you direct me?"

"Well, young man, I make the best cakes in the world but I'm not for hire. I'd suggest Mrs. Rosy Flannigan."

I'm sure my face falls, but I press on. "And where would I find Mrs. Flannigan and her bake shop?"

"Rosy is up on North Holland street. Robin's egg blue house, the only one it town. You can't miss it."

"Obliged, ma'am," I say, and return my hat.

"My pleasure," she says, as I hurry after Horace, now more than a half block ahead and striding. It looks to me like he's heading into the Stockman's Bank, but he passes the door and turns on the far side of the gray stone edifice.

I hurry past the bank and see a stairway heading up to a second-floor walkway. On the building, on that side, is a wooden sign mounted on the stone. In gold letters,

HARRINGTON LAND, CATTLE & MINING. An arrow points up the stairs. It seems the Harringtons have expanded their empire.

Now I know where Horace hangs his hat, and I presume daddy rules the kingdom from the same throne, so before I burn their world down, I should pay my respects to the former Rosy McDougle, now Rosy Flannigan. After things are even up, I might be hotfooting it to Oregon or California where there will be no posters bearing my ugly likeness nor a dollar amount encouraging my return to Deer Lodge or the nearest boot hill.

I wander back to Queeny's and recover Sand from the hitching rail, cinch him up and head slightly downhill, the way the kind direction-lady-in-the-bustle pointed. Two blocks beyond Stockman's Bank is North Holland Street, and I head uphill four blocks until I see a small robin's egg blue house with a brown roof of hand-split cedar shingles. The picket fence in front is also blue to match, but the hitching post is painted white. I guess Rosy ran out of blue, or I should say Mr. Flannigan ran out, whoever he may be.

I stroll up and rap on the door, bold as a tinsmith come to sharpen her knifes. The door's white to match the hitching post, and hear footsteps hurrying to answer. "I've got them ready," she calls out before opening the door, then does so with something steaming and wrapped in muslin in her arms.

Her eyes widen and I fear she's going to scream.

CHAPTER 9

SHE LOOKS, THEN TAKES A DOUBLE TAKE, THEN DROPS HER load. To my surprise, she steps over some fat rolls that are true to their name and rolling on the floor and throws her arms around me with a hug hard enough to take my breath. Then quickly she pulls me inside.

Is there a smell better than that of bread baking? Although I also caught a whiff of lilac from Rosy's hair, and that's nearly as appetizing.

She hugs me again, then pushes me away arm's length and stands with a hand on each of my shoulders. "Does Tuttle know your horse?"

"I don't think he knows I'm in town," I reply.

"He was here first thing and reported you'd escaped—word came by telegram—and asked me to be on the lookout for you. Does he know your horse?"

"Not unless he's been to Granite and talked to folks."

"He was headed there this morning to tell them to be on the lookout for you and a big black fella the wire said had escaped with you."

"He's at Kaiser's. I should warn him they're on to us."

"Do so, lay low and come back here via the alley. I'll feed you both." Then she looks a little worried. "He's safe to have around, no?"

"Yes, he's a fine fellow and a good friend. We'll be back ...." I start out and then turn back. "Mr. Flannigan won't give us up?"

"Mr. Flannigan is still deep in the Doodlebug Mine, and has been since a cave in three years past."

I grab my hat off again. "I'm sorry Rosy. Sorry for your loss, but not sorry he's not here at the moment."

"Well, Jack, he's not likely to be here ever again so come on back. I presume you can use a home-cooked meal."

"And a friend. And you're the only one I have on this earth, other than Jasper."

"Hurry off now. See you an hour after sundown. Leave your mounts tied down the block somewhere, so my house is not stormed by deputies."

"Stormed? How many are about?"

"Only two city—marshal and deputy. But there are four county, including the sheriff. Now go."

I run for my horse and keep to the back roads four blocks until I reach Cedar Street then head downhill to Kaiser's. But Jasper's big horse, Apollo, is not at either the side or front hitching rail. I don't want to risk riding the main street again, even though it's unlikely City Marshal Morgan Tuttle has had time to get to Granite and back. He may, however, have spread the word and now I know he's got a deputy. I do know the County Sheriff keeps his desk in the jail office next to City Hall, and I'm sure he's been informed of the escapees. With luck his deputies are spread all over the country. Still, not a good idea to say on P-Burg streets. Better I head back to our campsite, and better I not do so on the main road as I could come face to face with Tuttle. I want to settle up with the Harringtons first. Should they be sure I'm coming to Phillipsburg they could hire an army to protect them.

What little surprise I might have is my best friend at the moment. I believe it was General Grant said surprise is better than an extra regiment. So, I make it a couple of blocks past Broadway Street then veer off into the lodge-pole pines and work my way to our campsite through the forest.

Hell, it's a good time for a nap. But as I dismount, Jasper strides out of behind a thick pair of pines.

"Did you get your mountain oysters?" I ask.

"I did. Two servings. But don't get too comfortable as I saw some fella with a badge on the road. I got off a'fore he I came face to face with me, but I watched him stop on the road and study the way I'd ridden out. He headed on up toward Granite, but I wouldn't be a dang bit surprised he don't show back up with some help to track."

"Then we best put a trick on him. Let's go back to the road then ride the streambed uphill a ways. We got a supper date an hour after sundown with an old friend in town. So, let's stay alive and out of jail. You could use some home cooking?"

"Stuffed to the gills right now, but I'll be hungered come nightfall. Let's move out," he says, and we both mount up.

The road here is running north and south, and the stream south of us, but where it crosses the road is not far.

We're only a hundred paces from the streambed. It's a

fairly steep brook originating in the still snow-covered slopes high above. The stream is a couple of feet deep when running strong, but now only tumbles half-heartedly. It was cold last night so things likely froze up again, particularly higher up the mountain. I rein up Sand above the wagon road, more than a two track as I'm sure heavy freight wagons loaded with ore traverse it regularly. It's not so often as they did when Granite was at its peak, but still more than enough to keep any growth pounded down except for a small width of grass dead center.

I try to keep the buckskin on rocks until we reach the stream, then turn him upstream, east, when dead center. Jasper follows my example and we travel on the slippery rock bottom for a hundred yards before a six-foot waterfall forces us to move out and through a thicket until we find a good game trail to follow. I'm pleased that we're separated from the road by a thick stand of lodgepole pine as I hear riders—at least a half dozen. They're coming at a lope and it's obvious when they rein up. Even at this distance, we can make out voices, but not what's being yelled back and forth. I'm sure, however, they're hunting where Tuttle had seen a big black man rein off the road.

We're in a fairly sparse fir forest over a quarter mile from the road before I turn back north. I know there's another east-west road, an extension of Broadway Street, leading out of Phillipsburg. There after leaving town, it's called Tower Road as there are ore silos in a small mining area a couple of miles distant. When we cross Tower Road, I'll know exactly where we are.

"Hold up," Jasper says from behind me and I pull rein.

He cocks his head and listens, then turns back. "We didn't trick them ol' boys. I believe they're on our trail."

"Let's pick it up," I say spinning Sand back and giving him my heels. We don't have an easy way of it as there's quite a bit of blowdown. I'd planned to cross Tower Road and hide out in thick timber beyond. But if there's a half dozen on our tail, I'll have to take another tack and do. It's a steep drop down to Tower Road, and I'm leaning back so as to damn near have my head on Sand's rump by the time we make the road. Rocks continue to follow us down, bouncing, clattering, and coming to rest on the road.

Then I listen up. But Jasper and Apollo following are making so much noise I can't make anything else out.

As I suspected, the road's had plenty of traffic, so I turn west knowing town is only a mile or so distant. With the track of a hundred shod horses and a dozen wagons on Tower Road, it would take a Sioux Indian to follow our trail. I watch Jasper and Apollo plunge the last twenty yards through brush and rock outcroppings and am amazed when they light on the road unscathed.

I give him a chance to catch his breath, then yell at him. "Let's split up when we get to town and meet up a half mile on the other side. I'm going hell-for-leather until the outskirts, then let's go casual through town. Sit quiet a minute."

I cock an ear and swear I can hear hoofbeats and brush busting. We can't tarry.

CHAPTER 10

HE GIVES ME A NOD AS IF HE'S HEARD THEM ALSO. I SPIN Sand, and we are quickly at a gallop until I see the first of Phillipsburg's buildings, the stamping mill, and rein up to a casual trot. The pounding of shod hooves on a hard road can be heard for a long distance, as can the hard breathing and snorting of hard-ridden horses, but they'll quickly catch their wind. As soon as I pass the warehouse that marks the edge of town, I rein up and we keep a brisk walk. I turn up Cedar Street and pass the Kaiser. Jasper turns the other way for what I presume is a block, then back south. Again, under the circumstance, it won't do for us to be seen together. I move at least four blocks up and see the City Hall off to the south, the way I'm going anyway, so I laugh to myself. The last place they'd be looking for me is passing the City Marshal and Sheriff's office, and the jail.

So, cocky as a strutting rooster, with head held as high, I keep up a brisk walk right on past. I touch my hat brim and give a nod at a uniformed sheriff's deputy perched on the porch of the jail, but he barely looks up from rolling a smoke. I'm confident that Town Marshal Tuttle has not returned with a description of Sand, my buckskin. I hope he and whoever was riding with him turned east on Tower Road, thinking the last place we'd be going is into town if we were being trailed by a posse. There were tracks enough going both ways.

In minutes, I'm on the south side of the village, where another road heads east toward Anaconda then Butte; and the other way veers off northwest toward the Drummond Trading Post, on the Clark Fork River and many miles west of Deer Lodge Prison. On downstream from there, through Hell's Gate Canyon is Missoula. Upstream runs toward Butte, but the Continental Divide comes first. Climb into a canoe at Drummond and you can paddle west all the way to the Pacific, after joining up with the huge Columbia River north of the Canadian border. Head a few miles east, and all streams will take you to the mighty Missouri River. Your canoe will take you down it to St. Louis and the Mississippi, and downstream it to New Orleans and then the Gulf of Mexico.

I sigh deeply as Sand plods along, wishing I was in a canoe with Rosy, headed either way. After freezing every winter in Deer Lodge Prison, the sun in New Orleans or even rainy Oregon, or better yet, south to sunny California sounds pretty damn good. Sun, even in winter.

When I join up with the Butte-Drummond road, I see Jasper perched on a log aside the road a couple of hundred yards away and give him a wave. He quickly mounts Apollo and we ride toward each other. This side of town opens onto the wide Flint Creek Valley, almost totally fresh-green meadow grass except for reeds lining the creek that meanders through the valley. Both ways in the long valley, cattle bawl and graze. A half mile south of us, nearer the next range of mountains, a herd of a dozen mule deer grazes.

We have no place to hide while crossing the valley, except for the reeds. So, we head to the creek, cross it and picket pin the horses to graze. The reeds are tall enough to nearly hide the horses.

"You hungry," I ask Jasper as we plop down in the grass.

"Still full up with mountain oysters," he says, then offers, "I'll keep watch, you nap."

"You been going as long and hard as I have. I'll flip you for first nap."

"Heads," he says, and I dig a coin out and flip. It's tails, so I flop back in the grass, with tall reeds between me and town, which is a little more than a half mile away.

He shakes me awake, and by the sun, I can see I've been sleeping a couple of hours.

"Your turn?" I ask.

"Stay quiet. Four riders just came down that there Broadway Street and turned Drummond way on the road."

"Good," I say, and stretch and yawn. "I hope they go all the way there hunting us."

"I'm pretty sure they is the bunch what was on our trail. They stopped and one of them had one of them long telescope things, flashing brass-shiny in the sun, and took a long leisurely look out over the valley. He surely didn't make us as they rode on."

"Rode on to Hell is fine with me. You nap. Looks like we got about three hours to kill before we ride into Rosy's."

"Keep good look out, Jack. This here being free is settling in on me pretty damn good."

"Me, too. Sleep. Then we'll go to a home cooked."

He eyes me for a minute, then asks, "Then what, Jack? You gonna take them fellas down?"

I have to take a deep breath and let it out slow before I answer. "They owe me, and they got to pay."

"Don't know if'n I can be part of it. Like I said, I'm gettin' partial to being free. Don't get no mountain oysters in Deer Lodge."

"That's for damn sure. Nap. I'll keep a close watch."

I wake him when the sun touches the mountains to the west and the sky is saying good night with orange-rimmed clouds and sunrays shining up rather than down.

"Them fellas show back up?" he asks after sitting up.

"A pair of horsebackers with a woman riding astraddle—don't know what this world ls coming to. A buggy with a city-dressed fella. A dray pulled by a handsome four-up of matching sorrels with white feet, loaded with beer kegs. And a farm wagon full up with grain pulled by four rank mules that ain't been curried since birth. That's the traffic so far."

"We gonna take different ways back into town?" he asks.

"You bet. It's a robin's-egg-blue house with a matching picket fence, but we're to go in the alley way and tie our mounts off at least a half block away."

"Okay, but this lady don't know me, so you go in first and, if all's okay, give me a wave."

"Fine with me. Hell, you'd scare an army of Injuns away, they didn't know you like I do."

"You a funny fella," Jasper says, but knows I'm right.

We kill another hour after the sun drops below the horizon and when it's dead dark with about three-eighths of a waning moon, suck up the latigos on our mounts and head in. Before we reach the Drummond-Butte road, we split up.

Just to be cautious, I ride a half block past North Holland, but the town is quiet. A few oil lamps burn in windows, but were a seamstress to drop a pin, you could hear it. So, I cross back over North Holland to the alley. There's a church on the corner, windows all dark, but it has a hitching rail, so I tie up Sand and loosen his cinch so he can stand comfortable. It's beginning to warm up a little. A fella can't move as quickly as he might like in the long duster, so I roll it up and tie it behind the saddle before I head up the alley. I worry about leaving my Winchester but let it rest in its scabbard. My knife is there also, but I do keep my Colt on my hip.

I pause near Rosy's back gate and study the house. Two fruit trees, apples I think, flank the stepping stones and are beginning to leaf out. I hope she has some dried apples from last year for a pie. I'm as happy as I've been in seven years.

I listen for a minute and hear only the hoot of an owl and some violin squeaking somewhere in the distance. A dog barks a block away, but maybe at his own tail as I see no movement up that way.

Down the alley the other direction, I see a mounted man in the faded light from a nearby window. Jasper, right on time.

Heading for the door, I'm thinking about whistling a tune, but calling attention to myself is not wise.

Mounting Rosy's back stairs, I knock quietly. The

knob turns and the door opens just as two burly fellows round each corner, both with double barrel coach guns in hand. And when the door opens, it's not beautiful Rosy with warm dinner rolls in hand. It's City Marshal Morgan Tuttle with a double barrel leveled on my midsection.

"Howdy, Jack," he says, with a smug smile that I'd like to knock off his face, but I'm flanked and covered with six barrels of buckshot. He continues, "I hear you're going by Blackjack these days, at least up Granite way?"

I don't bother to reply, rather, I place both hands on top my hat and return the dumb smile. "I guess this means I'm gonna miss supper?"

As they're dragging me out, I can hear Rosy shouting, "They pushed their way in here, Jack. I didn't tell them nothing—not a dang thing! Somebody saw you leaving."

Her voice was shut off by the slamming of the door.

CHAPTER 11

COLD FLAT IRON BARS, SIX-INCH SPACING HORIZONTAL AND vertical, and a door made of the same heavy construction. Stone walls at least eighteen inches thick. And they won't be taking me out to work some mine or even to cut wood. Tuttle, with a crooked smile, informed me shortly after shoving me into this ten-by-ten-foot cell, that Deer Lodge was sending a prison wagon to transport me back. I've been in that wagon and I've about as much chance escaping from it as I do this rat cage.

I'm happy to note that Jasper is nowhere to be seen. Obviously, he wasn't caught up in the capture—or maybe I should say double cross. Now I'm really glad we came separately. I'm sure he was watching my capture from a front row seat.

I didn't miss my supper, not home cooked but a damn sight better than Deer Lodge gruel. A bowl of beans, a two-inch-thick slice of hot bread, and a couple of fat slices of hog back.

Tuttle is still giving me that crooked grin as he

watches me eat. When I've taken the last sop of bean juice with the bread, he gives a cackle then asks, "What the hell brought you back here, jackass? I figured anybody with half a brain would head for the mighty Mo and downstream on the first passing log."

I eye him for a long moment, then return his stupid grin and answer. "I figured lots of folks who hang their hats in Granite and here owe me as their lies cost me seven years."

He laughs again. "I guess a fellow would miss a lot— good fat steaks, poontang, a beer or shot of hooch now and again."

"Partly your fault, Morgan. You and all them that lied on the stand about me killing that sweet girl, Beth Ann."

"You still denying it?" he says. "You was the one giving her your wages for a poke every week."

"I hadn't seen her since I took up with another. It had been six months. And you know damn sure why I'm denying it, and you know Horace did the dirty deed."

"Well," he says with another grin, "It don't much matter now. Even if'n you didn't do the crime, you're doing the time."

"And what's Horace doing these days?"

Before he could answer, another voice rang out from the doorway to the outer office. "Why don't you ask me, Brannigan?" In walks Maxmillian Harrington his own self.

"Well," I say, with some growl in my voice, "if it ain't the black-hearted bastard himself."

"Watch your mouth or there won't be another bean for you before they haul your miserable ass back to the

Deer Lodge hole where you'll live for a few months. You're a damn fool, coming back here."

"I was hoping for a little taste," I say.

"Taste? Of what?"

"You're eyeballs, looking down the muzzle of my gun."

"Never gonna happen," Harrington says, then gives me a crooked grin.

"How's old Horace doing?" I ask. "Still turning on friends like a rattlesnake."

"He's doing just fine. I just put him on the stage over to Butte, and from there he's taking the Overland Express down to Ogden in Utah, then the Transcontinental and back to Washington, D.C. I guess you hadn't heard? Horace is to be the new Chief of Staff for Senator Wilburn."

"Bought him a job, did you? He damn sure didn't get one on merit."

"You're one to talk about merit, being a jailbird and all."

"Thanks to you buying lies from every lowlife worm like Tuttle who's willing to sell his rotten soul for a bit of coin."

"Don't blame Horace, Jack. He does exactly what I tell him to do. So does Tuttle. You live through the next years of your twenty-five-year to life sentence, should you get out for good conduct, unless you've likely bargained your chance away by escaping. If I'm still kicking when you are released, God willing, I'll have a decent job for you."

"Sorry, Max, but that don't make it right. Your boy's a murdering lout. If the law can't handle him, I can. Even if it's twenty years or more from now, I will throw dirt in his face. I'll tell you, even if I spend a good part of it in the hoosegow, I'll still live to piss on your grave. And I'll pour your whelp's blood on it for good measure."

"When pigs fly," he says, and laughs. On his way out I hear him snap at Tuttle, "Don't give the prick anything but bread and water tomorrow—not until the Deer Lodge wagon gets here. He's got way too much sass in him."

"Yes, sir," Tuttle says, and I hear the door close. And Tuttle yells at me, "Stick that bowl and spoon under the door, then go to the far side and plop your butt on the cot."

I do, and he fetches them. I can't help but dig him a little. "I thought you was the marshal, the stud duck in the city. Not a lowlife bean-servin'waiter. You muck the floors too?"

"You don't have to worry about it, Jack. I'll be locking you up tight and heading down to the Kaiser for a fat rib steak and then maybe beat bellies with a beautiful smooth-skinned sweet smellin' woman. You got the cockroaches to keep you company."

"I heard the only way you could beat bellies was to pay double for it. Who's got the duty tonight?"

"And maybe I'll nut you like a capon a'fore you leave for the hole so as to fatten you up for the slaughter. You don't need to worry about who's on duty. You won't need watching. Our jail is so tight even pond scum like you can't slip out. You got a pitcher of water, a thunder pot, and a blanket. I doubt it the place would burn even if I tried to light it up. So, I'm sorry to say, you'll likely be here when I check in tomorrow. Sheriff runs the jail, so he may show up first to make sure you ain't hung yourself ... or make sure you have." Then he laughs again, and adds, "How-some-ever should you want to forego your return trip to that stone hotel, I'll fetch you about six feet of hemp rope. That should do the job."

"I'll pass, thanks. If I stretched my neck, I wouldn't be able to come back here and tear your head off and piss your ears full."

"And I guess I could just shoot your dumb ass full of holes right now and say you reached through the bars and had ahold of my gun. How about that?"

"You better get along home before your cowardly ways take hold of you."

"Go to hell, Jack," he snaps, then slams the door between cells and office behind him. It's only moments when I hear the outside door slam.

I wait a while, then call out. "Tuttle!" and getting no answer call again.

He's gone and I'm locked up alone for the night. I search the cell over hoping to find a wire as part of the cot, or something I might try and use to pick the lock. But nothing. Hell, I might as well get some sleep, so I curl up in the blanket. I wish I had my duster, which I rolled up and left on the back of Sand's saddle. Thinking of Sand, I hope Jasper remembers to find and take care of him. I know Tuttle didn't as he, his deputy, and a sheriff's deputy hauled me straight from Rosy's to the hoosegow.

Something rattles and wakes me. I lie for a minute, listening, then hear a whisper. I can't make it out so I get up, then the shutters on the only window in the cell rattle. I hurry there and swing them open. There is no glazing, no glass, in the little two-foot-square window. It's covered by wooden shutters that open in, controlled by inside the cell.

"Them deputies gone?" It's Jasper's voice.

"Gone," I say.

A fat trace chain appears in the opening.

"Put it around," Jasper says in a harsh whisper, and I thread it around the four square bars keeping me inside. He hooks it together, closing the loop.

"Stand aside," he says, and I hear his footsteps on the gravel. Then the crack of a whip and the chain snaps taut. The whip cracks again, and I hear Jasper's voice. "Move that chain up and center it. Up team. Pull you black bastards." I pound the chain up center then have to smile to myself as I've heard him called the same many times by Fat Freddy Willard, one of the worst of the Deer Lodge guards.

The bars are bending slightly outward. But I fear the thick rock walls won't give even if his team is elephants. But the whip cracks again and the bars bend and one pops free, pulled from the grooves in which it rests top and bottom, then another, then the third—room enough.

I waste no time shimmying through the hole.

I'm impressed with the team of four big John mules.

"Where the hell?" I ask?

"Some drover drunk himself into a stupor and was rolled out in the back of his freight wagon. Som'bitch didn't even unhitch his team. So, I done helped him out."

"We afoot?" I ask.

"Hell no," he says, looking at me like I was a candle without a wick. "Our critters are tied up down at the church hitching rail. Let's go."

And I trot off behind him.

We reach the animals and mount up. Before he gives heels to Apollo, he eyes me like a bull at a bastard calf. "Can we get the hell out of here now. I'm thinking we head south, maybe all the way to Washoe Meadows. I hear Virginia City, Nevada Territory, has a hell of a strike and they keep on finding more."

"I'll ride across the valley with you, up into the Pintlers. You go on come morning, I appreciate you springing me and owe you, but I still got business here."

"And I thought you a quick learner," he says, then spins Apollo down toward the valley. "I will be going on. I ain't goin' back and you keep pressing our luck."

"I wish I could blame you, but I can't. I hope we meet again, both flush with coin, forgotten by the law, and in good health."

In an hour we're across the valley, having passed though cattle filled meadows and at least a hundred yards of Flint Creek flooded pasture, full of cattle tracks. It would take a formidable tracker to follow. I hear no one following, only the occasional bawl of a whiteface, a nighthawk screeching, and wind whistling through the cattails and meadow grass.

We ride to the top of the first small mountain, maybe five hundred feet above the Flint Valley, and make a dry camp in a thick copse of fir. Our bed's a foot-thick bed of needles and trash. Not goose down, but not a bit bad—a damn sight better than a cold stone bench in Deer Lodge.

I'm saddened by the thought of parting ways with Jasper as he's been a fine pard. He could have left me in that cold stone cell, but didn't. And he risked all to fetch me out.

Then again, it was my plan got him out of Deer Lodge.

I guess we're even up.

Now if we're not tracked until midmorning, Jasper can get a hell of a head start across the Pintlers, and I can plan my next move—whatever that may be.

CHAPTER 12

I'M A LITTLE SURPRISED AT MYSELF. YES, JASPER HAS become a friend, but if prison teaches you one thing, it's that every man is for himself. Maybe it's because we're out of prison that I started to depend on Jasper? Maybe it's because he sprung me when he could have been miles away and not risking his own freedom? Maybe it's because he decided to make the break with me, even though he only had a two-year stretch left? Whatever the reason, I actually choke up when bidding my buddy goodbye. He acts as if he hates us parting as well. Maybe we've begun to depend upon each other too much.

He's mounted, aimed up the mountain and turns back to me. "Blackjack, I know it's been a good spell for both of us without lady company, but don't let your need overcome y'all's caution again. I gonna be over the mountain and less'n you gots another friend, there ain't gonna be no chains and borrowed mules."

"I'll be careful."

"You don't get catched, you come on down Virginia City, Nevada, way and look me up. By the way, you still got your Winchester, but you might need this Colt more'n me?"

"No, sir. Tuttle took mine, but I intend to get it back and a pound of flesh."

"Be lot's more healthy to head out with me?"

"Get the hell out of here before that worthless Tuttle gets lucky and back on our trail."

Jasper shakes his head as if he's a little disgusted with me but smiles and touches his hat brim. Then he spins Apollo, and the big horse kicks rocks out behind as he heads for the very top of the mountain and soon, with luck, the Big Hole, then Idaho, then Nevada Territory and, soon after, he can follow the tracks of the Transcontinental all the way to a few miles north of Virginia City.

I yell after him, "Go with God, big man."

He waves again over his shoulder then disappears into a thick stand of firs, following a game trail half as wide as most Montana roads.

When he's gone from sight, I realize it's the first time in seven years I've actually been alone, when another man is not more than a few feet from me.

I'm relishing the silence, with only the chattering of squirrels, the singing of birds, and the breeze whispering through the thick firs. We've camped on the edge of a small meadow, now blooming with the bright yellow of Balsam Root Arrow Leaf, and some little white ones I think I remember are called snowflake flowers, but I'm not sure. I try to remember all Pete Stealhorse, my Blackfeet Indian fellow prisoner, taught me about what I could eat and what not to let touch my tongue. I have Sand staked out near a trickle coming from a spring at the base of a rock ledge, so I wander over his way. The trickle is lined with watercress, so I gather some up and munch on it for breakfast. Not much nourishment, but nice and fresh tasting none the less. The only greens we got at Deer Lodge were wild mustard, and them damn seldom and oft times undercooked and stringy.

Sand is the only friend I have left. I'm not even sure about Rosy, even though she claimed she was rushed by Tuttle, I have no real way of knowing she didn't invite them to gather me up when I had my mind on a home-cooked meal, and hopefully a little female companionship—and I don't mean small talk over supper. Hell, maybe there was even a reward already out for us.

So, I turn to my only friend, "What do you think, Sand, old partner. Do we go back to Phillipsburg?"

The buckskin paws at the ground, then goes back to grazing. I take that to mean we go back, but not until we got the cover of darkness.

"Good idea, Sand," I say, and he nickers then goes back to grazing.

I still have a handful of jerky in my saddlebags, and a single chunk of hardtack. I'm happy to see my hunting knife—actually Fat Freddy Willard's hunting knife—is still there. Had I been thinking, I'd have added to my take from Corny, a side of bacon, some beans, some coffee, salt and sugar, and a pot or two. But what the hell, I've seen a half-dozen whitetail deer down close to the valley floor, at least that many mule deer up here on the higher slopes, and, at a distance, a whole herd of elk.

Pulling Sand's picket pin, I move him a few feet where he has fresh graze and can still reach the trickle.

My saddle with the Winchester in its scabbard is across a rock and I wander over and pull the rifle, dig my knife out of the saddle bag, then turn back to Sand. "I got a hankering for a chunk of tenderloin. Don't get nervous and pull that pin," I say, then strike off across the meadow.

I haven't gone three hundred yards, traversing the mountain, when I spot a fat mule deer which seems to have wintered well. And she's grazing with twin yearlings. A doe and a spike buck. I likely don't have time to mess with a full mule deer carcass, so I eye the spike. I'm downwind from them so I move closer until my shot is no more than one hundred yards. If one doesn't want to be discovered, he doesn't shoot more than one time. One time and whoever hears it only knows there's been a shot, it's the second shot that gives you direction.

My first shot knocks the spike down hard, without even a kick. Mama and her big doe fawn run into the trees and I plop down on the stump of a ponderosa that the lumberjacks took several years ago, and wait. The spike went down like a dropped sack of potatoes, but I've had them come to and get their legs under them. I don't want to go on a chase, so I wait to make sure Mr. Spike has drawn his last breath.

Besides, I want to make damn sure no one has heard the shot and is climbing the mountain to see who was plunking away. Even with one shot they could get lucky.

So, I walk to an outcropping where I can see down the mountain, all the way across the valley and Flint Creek, to Phillipsburg.

Nothing but cattle.

In another half hour I have liver, heart, backstraps, tenderloins, and a hindquarter wrapped in my shirt.

With flint and steel I have a fire of blowdown burning

down to coals, and soon have heart, liver, and a fat chunk of hindquarter skewered on a willow branch and turning over a bed of glowing embers. More than I can eat, but it'll keep in my saddlebags for a good spell, and I'll likely be on the run.

Tomorrow is another day. When it comes, about a half hour after midnight, I'll wander on down to Phillipsburg and see what's to find and pocket at Harrington Land, Cattle & Mining. They sure as hell owe me something, and with luck, Max Harrington, his very own self, will wander in and try to stop me.

With luck.

CHAPTER 13

I REALIZE WHEN I RIDE IN THAT IT'S SATURDAY NIGHT, AND town is busy even at half past midnight. I hitch Sand to a small tree a half block up the side street from the bank and Harrington's office and make my way there on foot.

Careful I'm not being seen, I stay in the shadows until no one is near on Broadway.

The stairway up beside the bank to Harrington Land, Cattle & Mining tops out on a wide landing. There's a thick door leading into the offices, but it's flanked by two windows each with a dozen smaller panes of glass. Both are casement—push-up style. A small tap breaks a pane. I'm able to jimmy the clasp and raise the bottom half enough to slip in and quickly close it.

There's a line of windows as large as those flanking the door facing Broadway and a busy saloon and pleasure house across the wide street. It's well-lit and throws slivers of light so I can make my way around the office without striking a Lucifer. At the back of the office rests a safe that likely equals the one in the bank below. In fact, I wonder how the floor can support it. I'm not going to find out what it contains without a wagon load of dynamite, so I ignore it and keep looking. Four desks occupy the main office and I search every drawer in them. My take is a small bag of hard candy and a two-shot belly gun, a Derringer by make I'd guess but will have to have more light before I can tell. A box of .44 caliber cartridges tells me its knockdown power, so I pocket both.

I hope I have better luck in the back office and when I move to that door, I see it's marked in gold letters "Maximillian P. Harrington, Proprietor." And the door is not locked. The desk inside is the size of a billiard table, only a slight exaggeration. Off to a side is a glass case on a nicely polished oak or hickory stand. When I get next to it, I get a wide grin. Four gold nuggets rest inside; one the size of my fist, the other three smaller but still impressive.

As breaking the glass can't be done without some noise, I decide it will be done just before I exit. Even with the constant clank and rumble of the ore crusher in the distance, a continual background noise, the smashing of thick glass might be heard.

This big desk has two locked drawers. I try to jimmy the wide desk above the knee space with my knife, but it's stubborn so I go back to the outer office, recover a screwdriver I'd noted in one of the other desk drawers and return.

I'm much more enthusiastic with the screwdriver and bust the drawer away from the desk top. Inside dead center is a fat envelope marked Friday. And inside Friday is a thick slab of paper money, a dozen twenty-dollar double eagles, and twice that many ten-dollar gold pieces. That, too, brings a smile. I'll count it later, but

Friday must be a good day at whatever Harrington business supplied it. The side drawer, big enough for files, is a little tougher to break and I bend the screwdriver before it gives. Files, and no more envelopes—I was hoping for Monday through Thursday—but almost as welcome is a beautiful engraved Navy Colt in a fine black holster on a black cartridge-filled belt and a box of .44/.40 cartridges. I now am well heeled.

If I didn't want blood from the Harringtons, this and the nuggets, would do nicely. But I fear it's not enough to worry them more than minor irritation. So, revenge is still on my list of to do's.

I use the butt of the Colt on the thick glass protecting and showing off the nuggets and it does make some considerable noise. I'm now loaded down, Winchester in one hand, heavy nuggets, coins, and paper money in my duster pockets, and a new gun belt and Colt on my hip.

It's all I can do not use my Lucifers to start a conflagration and burn the Harrington headquarters out, but with the bank below and likely half the town being dreadfully injured by the loss of it, I bite the bullet and ease my way out the window. As quietly as I can toe, I make my way down the stairs.

"Far enough," a hard voice rings out as I reach the shaded boardwalk on the bottom. "What the hell are you up to," the voice repeats, and I recognize Deputy Morgan Tuttle. I'm in the shade of the landing above, and I sense he's yet to recognize me.

"Cleaner," I say, in as deep a voice as I can muster.

"Bullshit," Tuttle says. "In a duster? The hell you are, I got you covered. Step out here where I can see you."

I have a cartridge chambered in the Winchester, but he's

drawn and leveled on me. Still, I ain't going back. So, I step forward and cock the rifle as I do. He drops the hammer on his rifle and I should be dead, but nothing. He looks at it like he's not hearing right, then I see his eyes flare as he recognizes me. He obviously hadn't levered in a shell, but now he does. We fire at the same time and I'm spun around and slammed back into the railing I'd stepped around. It keeps me from going to my back. I grab for my side and realize I'm hit, but below the rib cage and above the hip bone.

Morgan Tuttle is not so lucky. My slug took him dead center between the tits and I surmise through his black heart. He hit hard on his back and has not twitched.

Light floods the street as the bat wings on the saloon across the way are being held open. Wound or no wound, I've got to pick them up and put them down. I round the corner of the bank building and as quickly as I can—holding my Winchester in my right hand and my side with my left—make my way up the side street to Sand. I scabbard the rifle and have some trouble getting into the saddle but do. My heads swimming from the effort and I wonder for a moment that I might take a dive into the street. But I collect myself and give Sand my heels.

I've got to find a place to hole up and heal up, and only know of one household I can be sure of. Suttervilles. My Pa's old mine and the folks who now work it.

If I can get there.

I rein Sand up and around town to the west side, then turn him up hill toward my pa's old mine. I have to reconcile in my mind that I've likely killed a man. You don't live through a dead center chest shot with a .44/.40. I guess I should be worried about my eternal soul, but I have to believe that part about 'thou shalt not kill' doesn't apply to self-defense, but only by the grace of God—and Tuttle's stupidity—am I not strapped to a plank and displayed dead as a cow patty and leaned up against the post office for all to see.

It's dawn, and I wonder if I'll live to see another, when, with mighty effort and hours of pain, I make it up the mountain to where Henry and Maggy Jane have a warm spot and some hot food.

I rein up in front, and Sand neighs loudly. I'm laying down on his neck and it's likely he's more than ready to get shed of me.

The door opens and Henry's already dressed for the mine. He has a double barrel in hand, but quickly leans it aside, and yells to his wife. "Maggy, it's George Horseman, and he's hurt."

As he's helping me from the saddle I remember the alias I gave him. I mutter to him as he helps me inside. "Henry, actually it's Jack Brannigan, should you need to carve a marker."

"Stay quiet while Maggy patches you up. Water?" he asks as he plops me on their dining table and lays me out and strips away my duster and shirt.

"Through and through," he says. "I'll get my cleaning rod."

And damn if I don't know what that means. He's gonna swab the wound like he was cleaning his barrel. I manage one request as Maggy Jane shows up with her sewing basket.

"Jug?" I ask, and in seconds Henry is at my side and I'm swigging and coughing his homebrew corn. I'm cross-eyed drunk when he goes to work with a whisky-soaked swab.

But not cross-eyed enough. I'm embarrassed as I think I might have awakened the dead with my yell. Maggy goes to the wood bin and returns with a one-inch-thick branch and invites me to chomp down, which I do. I presume my moans are bothering her in her work.

I must have passed out as I awaken and Henry is long gone, In the mine I suppose. I'm on a pallet of bedclothes in front of the fire. The smell of something cooking makes my mouth water and I turn. Almost as quickly, Maggie Jane is by my side with a mug of water.

"Glad you done woke up," she says, and flashes white teeth at me. "Gots you some broth cooking."

"Sand?" I ask, and she looks a little confused, so I add, "my horse."

"Grained and watered and in the barn. You r... possessions ..." she says and seems a little awed, "is hidden out there, too. You been doin' right well. I don't suppose the law is on your tail?"

"I suppose they are. I'll be going ...."

"No, sir. You'll be healing up. Our dogs'll come out from under the porch and go to barking if'n riders are coming and we'll hide you and your horse out in the mine. Now I'm gonna fetch you some broth." Then she turns back to me. "Where's that other fella was with you?"

"Said he was headed out of the territory."

She nods and takes the mug to her stove and ladles in some broth. And it's about the best thing I ever tasted. Then she gives me a tight grin. "You're lucky I'm a fine hand with a needle. You might want another pull or two on the jug as you're needing some stitching, front and back."

I compliment myself for coming to the right place. I take a cup of broth and, with lots of teeth gritting, am soon sewed up like a rag doll, and asleep again.

CHAPTER 14

THANKFULLY IT'S MY THIRD DAY AT SUTTERVILLES BEFORE the dogs start raising hell. I've just been able to get to my feet and out to the privy and back this morning for the first time, and that with the help of a crutch.

The Seth Thomas clock on Maggy Jane's wall says nearly noon. About how long it would take for riders to reach the mine from Phillipsburg had they left first thing in the morning.

Maggy Jane hands me a walking stick and points me to the mouth of the mine, forty yards and uphill at least ten.

"Go," she commands, and I hobble with gritted teeth as my side feels as if Henry is running that swab through it again. She disappears around the corner, yelling over her shoulder, "I'll bring your horse up. Give a yell when you get there and fetch Henry out."

Actually, Maggy Jane beats me to the mine, leading Sand. Hand on Sand's rump, I follow them in, hearing her yell for her husband, "Somebody coming, Henry. Henry, get out here."

She abandons me when we're fifty feet into the darkness. Far ahead, a lantern glows and it's coming closer until I make Henry out. He doesn't pause to visit but rather hurries on past, instructing me as he does, "Stay quiet. Keep your animal quiet."

"Yes, sir," I say, and, with great effort, pull my shirt off to muffle Sand if need be. Then I wait.

It seems twice as long a time as actual, as I was on my feet for the first time this morning and just staying on my feet is a job. I feel it in my side and as if I'm about to pass out. I have to plop my butt down on the mine floor. I figure I'm here nearly a half hour, when Sand decides he's had enough of a mine and jerks loose from my grasp —easily done—and trots for the opening.

I can't imagine what some dang posse will think seeing a buckskin horse trot out of a mine entrance. I struggle to my feet and consider hobbling deeper into the mine, but hell, a one-legged man could catch me the way I'm moving. I lean back on the rough stone wall and wait.

It's only moments when Henry appears. "You ain't much of a horse wrangler, Jack. Or is it Blackjack?"

I smile feebly. "Some were calling me that after I had a run at a table in Granite."

"They gone. They was hunting you. Come on out in the good light and I'll show what they think of you, Blackjack."

Following him out, I finally make the entrance and he has a one-foot by one-and-a-half-foot or so poster. It's a flyer on Jack 'Blackjack' Brannigan, and I must say I wish I looked as much the killer as the line drawing above the typeset. The drawing shows a fella with a full head of shoulder-length hair and four-inch beard. I have to smile.

The type reads:

WANTED

DEAD OR ALIVE

$300.00 Reward

Jack 'Blackjack' Brannigan

Murder, Jail Break, Prison Break

Shot a City Marshal in Cold Blood.

Known to trade coats with negro

Jasper Todd Jefferson ($100 reward).

May be attempting to sell seven pounds of

gold nuggets and in possession of an engraved

ivory handled .44/.40 Navy Colt. Known to carry it

and a 73 Winchester. Buckskin gelding.

WHEN I FINISH READING, I'm smiling, but Henry is not.

"Shot that City Marshal down in cold blood, did you?"

"Henry, he laid down on me with a Winchester and pulled one off. Luckily the damn fool didn't have one in the chamber. He levered in, and I had no choice. Shoot or die. We shot at the same time and I guess my aim was better than his."

Henry nods and is quiet for a minute. "And them nuggets, coin and paper money you got. That I got hid in the barn for you."

"Colonel Maximillian P. Harrington bought a jury and that City Marshal—a county deputy at the time up in Granite—and they lied, and I went to prison. It was

Harrington's worthless son killed the lady—the murder they hung on me."

"That don't explain the gold and coin."

"I figured Harrington owed me for the seven years I've already done, so I busted into his office and lifted the nuggets he was showing off, the money, and a fine Colt revolver."

"Okay, I know about that Harrington som'bitch. Let's get you back to that pallet and get you well so we can get shed of y'all, much as we enjoy your company." He smiles for the first time.

"You think they'll be back?"

"Doubt it. Maggy Jane and I are pretty good with the tall tales. We asked for one of them posters they were carrying to put up aside every road and trail saying we'd sure like to have that three hundred you're worth."

I laugh. "That's steep room and board, but I'll pay it."

"A dollar a day will do, now that you're in the money. Maggy's cooking is worth more, but that's what's fair. You're bleeding a little, weeping from that hole in your back. Get your damn shirt on so's y'all is decent and let's get you back down to rest up. Rest is what you need, and Maggy Jane's cooking. I believe it would cure a leper."

I nod, pull my shirt back on, and he gives me a shoulder to lean on to get back inside.

I'm with them for another three days and figure at damn near a week, I've pressed my luck enough. Not for my own good, but for theirs. Was I discovered here, I fear it wouldn't go well for them, so I'm riding out. Maggy Jane says she'd like me to wait another few days so she can pull my catgut stitches, but I thank her and say I can pull the front ones and will find another Florence Nightingale to pull the back few.

With a poster on every road and trail, even one showing me looking like a wild man from Borneo, I'm not heading back to Phillipsburg until things quiet down and those flyers have rotted off trees, walls and fence posts.

Now that I have pounds of gold nuggets, three hundred dollars in gold coin, and seven hundred sixty-two dollars in paper money, I'm heading where I have business but won't be recognized—Washington, D.C.

If I can get out of Montana Territory without getting shot dead for the reward.

It's Wednesday evening and Maggy Jane has an elk roast in the oven, potatoes and onions in the fry pan, and a huckleberry pie with berries she's reconstituted from dried. It will be my last supper with them.

Henry comes in from the mine, cleans up, and asks me if I think I'm ready to share three fingers of his good corn liquor. The three of us take a seat at their table. I roll out one of the smaller nuggets, maybe a third the size of my fist, on the table.

"I appreciate what you've done for me. I owe you and want you to have this chunk of yellow."

"Too much," Henry says.

"Maybe you think so, but I think my life is worth lots more. So, you're keeping this. That said, you got to melt her down to a bar or two, as the former owner might recognize it if not."

"Former owner?" Maggy Jane says, and gives me a hard look, then adds, "Can't take no stole goods."

"Believe me, Maggy Jane, he owed me so he may

think it stolen, but it was owed. Henry knows the whole story."

"Far as I'm concerned," Henry says, "It's Jack's money to give."

Maggy Jane shrugs her shoulders. "You say so, Mr. Sutterville. Good enough for me."

"I'll be riding out first light." Then I give them a smile and add, "However, that nugget includes the cost of a haircut and shave. As it is, I look a little too much like some hooligan on a bunch of posters."

They laugh, and Maggy Jane asks, "After supper or in the morn?"

"After supper. I'll even help with the dishes."

"You'll lay down and catch your breath."

"Yes, ma'am. Can I finish this good dollop of corn first?"

"What kind of hostess would I be, Mr. Blackjack?" I love that smile of Maggy's.

I figure I've still got five and a half pounds of nuggets in the three remaining. That's eighty-eight ounces of gold at sixteen dollars the ounce in the rough. Maybe more as unique large nuggets sometimes bring extra due to their display interest. That's at least one thousand four hundred dollars. That, plus the coin and the paper should get me to our nation's capital in high style.

I'm not feeling guilty as what I figure is a total of just over two thousand four hundred dollars is less than a dollar a day for the time I spent in Deer Lodge.

CHAPTER 15

SAND IS A FINE HORSE AND I'LL HATE PARTING WITH HIM when I have to transfer to a stage in Virginia City, which I'm now on the outskirts of. It's been two days of hard riding, making over sixty miles a day. I've had the occasional nausea from my wound, but less and less, hour by hour.

Virginia City, Montana, is a typical mining strike town, now ten years in the making. Bank, opera house, a half dozen saloons, and unlike Phillipsburg the ore crusher is far enough out of town the residents don't have to tolerate the crunch of rock day and night.

No one pays much attention to Sand and me as we clomp into town. I make note of the nicely whitewashed Wells Fargo & Co. Overland Mail and Express Office, which is my destination, but my stomach says café, so I keep riding. There's a hostler next to Ruby Chang's Café, Holland's Horses and Wagons, so I stop there first. It's a half dollar to water, grain, and groom Sand. I agree. I haven't mentioned selling him, and won't until he looks his best.

I do not leave my saddlebags with the livery even though Mr. Holland looks to be an honest gent. With saddlebags over a shoulder containing my new riches, I hunt a stomach full.

Despite the Asian name, Ruby's serves good old Montana grub and I invest another half dollar in a fat steak, eggs, coffee, toasted bread, jam, fried taters and onions.

Before I find a new home for Sand, I head to Overland and find the stage will leave for the south in the morning. I barely glance at the poster among a half dozen other announcements posted on a board outside. Happy to note that Blackjack fella has black hair to his shoulders and a full unkempt beard.

"Your name, sir?" the express company clerk asks as he issues me a ticket. Five days to Ogden, Utah, and the Transcontinental station, where another one hundred dollars will get me a Pullman sleeping car first-class ticket to Washington, D.C.

"Thad Johnson," I say, the first name that comes to me.

"Any relation to Hanford Johnson? Has a claim down Alder Gulch."

"Not that I know of," I return his smile. Then ask, "I've got a fine six-year-old buckskin gelding I need to sell, and I'm partial to him and want him to have a good master and facilities."

"We're always ...."

"No, no sir. He's earned an easier life than hard runs of fifteen or more miles pulling coach every day."

"We treat our animals ...."

"Good, I know. Any other ideas for me?"

"Willoby, the preacher over at the Presbyterian Church was in yesterday, looking for a retired coach horse. He no longer rides but needs a buggy horse."

"Sounds good. Where exactly?"

"You need a place for the night?"

"I do."

"The church is just beyond the Virginia City Inn, where you can get a clean bed and hot bath. West three blocks. Willoby's in the cottage next to the creek just behind the church."

"Saw it on the ride in."

"Don't be late. Sandy will whip up the team at 7:00 a.m. sharp. You forfeit your ticket less'n your aboard."

I tip my hat and head back to Holland's.

Mr. Holland takes my half dollar and asks, "You're taking the stage, so are you wanting to sell your buckskin?"

"And tack," I reply.

"I can give you thirty dollars for the animal and another five for the tack."

"Thanks. I may want to take you up on the saddle and bridle but, I may have a home for the buckskin." He's a fifty-dollar animal and the rest is worth ten at least, but I understand a man having to make a profit. Fact is, I want the best possible home for Sand.

I saddle up and head out for Willoby's. On approaching, I surmise that If the pastor keeps his animals like he keeps his grounds Sand will get fine care. Daisies are already blooming along the stepping stones to his front door, and wild roses are nicely planted and trimmed and beginning to bloom on the white picket fence separating yard from road.

"I lost my old mare this past week," the well-groomed gray-headed preacher says. "She was eighteen. What do you have to have for the buckskin?"

"He's worth fifty or more. Holland offered me thirty. As I want him to have a good home I'll take the thirty."

He gives me a trader's smile. "I'll have to train him to the buggy."

"He's a quick learner."

"How about twenty."

"Twenty-five, and you ask the Good Lord for forgiveness for taking advantage of a poor traveler."

He laughs. "Twenty-five it is."

Next door to Ruby Chang is a tailor. As I've never had tailor-made clothes since my ma sewed them and dressing decent would be as good a disguise as any for a prison escapee, I decide to give him a chance at me. Errol Lee is a half-Chinese, half-Englishman gent with a constant smile and ample waistline, I discover after a few minutes chat. He'll custom fit me for a suit of clothes of the latest fashion and have them ready by 5:00 a.m., for the princely sum of five dollars. We reach a bargain when I get him to throw in a fine white shirt, arm garters, and a four-in-hand silk tie. I'll don a cutaway coat, waistcoat, and matching trousers in the morn. For another dollar, from the mercantile, I acquire a pair of black brogans, then add underwear, socks, a comb and straight razor, small strop to sharpen, and brush and mug of shaving soap. Not confident the tailor will fit me tightly, I acquire a pair of soft leather suspenders. To top it off, I add a small carpetbag for my belongings. The bag has a hidden pocket inside which fits the Derringer I lifted. Come tomorrow morning, I'll look like a banker, undertaker, or preacher—anything but an escaped convict. To round out the disguise—and my new high-class appearance—I stop at the tonsorial parlor for a professional haircut and shave. I leave smelling like a flower for the first time in my life.

If the sheriff discovered my identity, walked in and shot me dead, I'd now be in fine fettle for my pine box.

The inn, as the Overland clerk promised, is a clean room, hot bath, supper and breakfast included for six bits, bath fifteen cents extra. I'm flush and go for the full treatment, although I'll be leaving before the 7:00 a.m. breakfast is served. McMannis, the innkeeper, promises me a bacon and egg sandwich at 5:00 a.m. I'm happy to discover the room includes a wind-up alarm clock with a ring as shocking as if a rattlesnake was between your legs.

As I sit at a large ten-seat table for a pot roast supper, I'm joined by six other guests. Two drummers, an older couple travelling through, a mining engineer, and a gentleman whose company I'm not particularly happy to have—the county sheriff. Sheriff Paddy O'Malley is a fellow who has never missed a meal and I'm happy to say doesn't require much conversation as he shovels it in. But he gets curious when he finishes well before I do. I would pick a place that serves as home for a lawman.

"So, what brings you to town?" he asks, smoothing his generous handlebar mustache as he talks.

"Wells Fargo Stage, transferring to the Overland," I reply, keeping it as succinct as possible.

"Where from?" he asks, pressing.

"Fort Benton, most recent. Been shopping for a little ranch to purchase or homestead."

"Did you meet Anthony Sutton, land agent, up Fort

Benton way?" he asks, after a sip of coffee, studying me carefully over the rim of his cup.

Ignoring his question, I reply, "To be truthful, I decided the country was too cold for my taste."

"So, where now?"

"Nevada," I lie. "You're a curious sort, Sheriff O'Malley." I give him a disapproving glance.

"Part of the job, mister. What did you say your name was?"

I have to pause a second to remember the name I gave the Overland clerk, and luckily only hesitate a moment. "Jackson. Up on the riverboat from St. Louis."

"Which boat?" he asks.

As I have no idea the name of any riverboats on the Missouri, I grab a name out of the air, one I'd name my boat should I have one. "Black Swan. Sidewheeler. One hundred fifty feet long, thirty-foot beam, loaded with every kind of goods you can imagine." I'm looking him right in the eye, convincingly.

"Must have been the first boat of the season?" he asks.

I stretch my arms wide, and yawn. Shrug, but don't answer, treating his question as if it was a comment. "It's been a long hard day. I believe I'll excuse myself." The cook is standing in the kitchen door, so I rise and turn to her. "Great feed, ma'am. Thank you." Then turn back to the table. "Night y'all," spin on my heel and head for the stairway.

"Close-mouthed fella," I hear the sheriff say to the others as I reach the base of the stairs. Then he questions, "Anybody see what he's riding?"

One of the drummers replies, "Came in on the stage from Helena, I believe."

I'm happy he's wrong, but convincingly so. At the moment it's a good thing some fellas want to sound right, even if wrong.

Morning, with the eastern sky just showing some silver, I'm on time to the tailor, who's worked the night through. Then, nattily dressed, to the stage, with a bacon and egg sandwich in my duster pocket. Sandy, the driver, and Alabama, the shotgun guard, seem fine fellas.

I'm happy to see Virginia City pass and disappear behind as Sandy cracks a whip and yells "pull" at the six up.

And even more pleased to note I'm accompanied by a redheaded lass who's as comely than any I've had the pleasure to admire.

CHAPTER 16

As travelers in close quarters are apt to do, we make introductions all around before we've gone a mile. I decide it's again time for a name change. "Brad Jackson," I say, extending my hand to a full-bearded, rough-looking fella who looks to be a trapper or buffalo hunter.

He shakes, and offers, "Porter Polkinghorn, down from the high lonely."

Then I turn to another nattily dressed fella in a herringbone suit and brocaded waistcoat. "Slade," he offers, and we shake. I swear it's a diamond stickpin in his black silk four-in-hand tie.

A buxom woman, gray-haired, with pince nez glasses is between them, ramrod straight, but looking a little seasick from the swaying coach and eying me like I was a carbuncle on her husband's backside. "Ma'am," I say, and she nods.

"Mrs. Martha Sniddleman," she offers, but it obviously pains her to do so.

Finally, I turn to the demure redhead on my right. "Ma'am. I'm Brad Jackson."

"Mr. Jackson. Miss Mary Ann Merriweather. Nice making your acquaintance." Then she turns to the others, and adds, "Nice to be travelling with you folks. I'm off to a teaching position in Oakland."

"Going home to Missouri to settle my folks' estate," Polkinghorn, the trapper, offers.

"Salt Lake City to join my husband," Mrs. Siddleman says and dabs at her nose with a lace hanky.

We all eye the man with the diamond stickpin, until he speaks up. "Just travelling."

"And you, Mr. Jackson," the redheaded lass asks.

"Going east. My business in the west is finished. At least some of it," I say.

I notice the fella who looks like a riverboat gambler is heeled with a small Derringer, much like mine, in a waistcoat pocket. The trapper has a large revolver at his side. He's removed it and rolled it in a cartridge belt at his side.

"Unusual sidearm?" I ask him.

"A Lefaucheux, M1858," he offers, then adds, "made in France. I carried it during the recent unpleasantries. I don't suppose you'd be related to Stonewall?" he asks, then adds, "God rest his soul."

"God curse his rotten soul," the gambler snaps, and the two glare at each other.

"Gentlemen," Mrs. Siddleman quickly steps in. "The war is long behind us. Let's leave it there."

"Humph," the trapper says, but turns and stares out the window.

It's obvious he's a southern man and the gambler's sympathies are with the victor. This may be a very long trip if these two are to be at each other's throats. I'm happy Mrs. Sniddleman is between them.

"Did you participate in the war?" the trapper asks me.

I decide it's a subject best left behind, so merely turn and watch the country go by.

"You didn't answer?" Mary Ann Merriweather asks, directing her question to me.

I clear my throat before replying. "Well, ma'am, I was a bit young to participate."

"What business did you have here in Montana Territory?" she asks.

I guess I should be complimented that she's interested, but prefer to remain a little elusive, at least until I've left Montana far behind. However, I feel compelled to answer, so I create a story. "I represent some folks back East who are interested in farm and ranch land out this way."

"My, how interesting," she says, and I feel a little guilty for my falsehood.

It's to be five or six stage stations each day, fifteen or more or less dusty, grimy, bouncing, teeth-rattling miles between each, depending upon the terrain. At most stops, we can only stretch while teams are rapidly changed. We lay over midday for soup and biscuits, then for the night for stew and baked bread, then breakfast of mush, eggs, or Johnny cakes and molasses. Sleeping conditions are fine for men, but not the best for ladies. Bunks and little privacy, privies out back, a room with temporary privacy to disrobe and beat the dust from garments. Common bone-white bowls and pitchers, with luck, a looking glass to wash up and tuck hair back in the dust caps the women wear.

Late on the second day in the black lava rock country north of the old Oregon Trail at Fort Hall on the Snake River, ninety miles from the last stop at the Dubois Stage Stop and trading post, I'm surprised to hear Sandy the driver yelling "whoa," and pulling rein. I roll up the dust cover on the window and stick my head out to see a fella with a saddle slung over his shoulder who's walking up as if he needs to catch a ride. It's a hell of a place for a fella to be afoot as this black-rock country is torture on man and beast.

"Horse went lame," I hear him call out.

Sandy climbs down and walks a few feet to meet the man, and relieves him of his saddle. Alabama, the shotgun guard, as is the custom, stays in his seat at the ready.

I glance back and am surprised to see three other fellas appear out of one of the deep clefts in the rock, running forward.

"Look out!" I yell, reaching for my Colt, but it's too late.

Another owlhoot has appeared on the far side of the coach and has jerked the door and has a coach gun panning all of us inside.

I show my hands, not wanting to have half me blown out onto the road.

The first one has palmed his revolver and is shouting. "Grab a weapon and die. There are two more sharp-shooters out in the rocks. If'n we don't kill you, they will, so don't give us a reason."

"Unload, pilgrims," the one who holds the shotgun demands, and we do.

The trapper leaves his revolver, still in its holster still

rolled in its belt, on the seat. Slade buttons his coat, hiding his Derringer, but complies and climbs out. I follow and the shotgun robber grabs my Colt from under my coat as I pass.

The first robber who acted as a stranded traveler, yells up to Alabama, who has yet to give him his coach gun. "Throw down the coach gun then the box, ugly."

I look up to see he has the shotgun leveled on the stranded traveler. His voice, answering, is low and gravelly. "Mister, this box and these travelers are placed in my trust and I've sworn to protect them. Both these barrels is cocked, and even should you or them other lowlifes pull off and shoot me in the ticker, I'll likely cut you in half. So, if'n I was you, I'd just ride on out and leave us be."

The shotgun robber who is covering us passengers is panning the muzzles back and forth. He has no clear shot at the shotgun guard, nor do four other robbers who are all spread across the road at the rear of the Concord.

It's a bit of a standoff, so I break the silence. "Hell, I probably got as much in my carpetbag as the Overland has in that money box."

CHAPTER 17

U<small>NLIKE MOST THE OTHERS,</small> I <small>HAVE MY BAG SHOVED UNDER</small> the seat inside the coach, so I ask the one covering me, "Hey, pard, you got my gun. You want I should get my bag and my stash?"

"Get it," he says, then adds, "we'd a got around to all you and your riches. Watch it, you'll get both barrels you try something."

"All I want is for all of us to get on about our business," and I reach inside and drag the bag out. As I do, I whisper to Slade. "Let's solve this," and he gives me the slightest nod.

I turn to the shotgun robber. "I'm gonna open this and shake out my gold."

"Do it," he snaps.

I loosen the ties on my bag, open it and turn it upside down, dumping my rough clothes, shaving gear, and the rest of my goods on the rock road, including my poke with the gold coin and paper money.

"Here you go," I say, and kick the poke the ten feet between us. At the same time, I'm fishing my Derringer out of the little hidden pocket in the bag. The shotgun bandit bends to grab up the bag, and I cock and fire the first barrel of the pocket gun, hitting him in the top of his head and dropping him flat on his face like the splat of a road apple out of one of Sandy's mules.

One of his two barrels fires, but goes astray, blowing out one of the spokes on the rear left wheel of the Concord.

I dive for the shotgun and my Colt, now stuffed in the dead bandit's belt, and hear another shotgun roar behind me. I presume that's Alabama.

As I'm grabbing up the bandit's shotgun, Slade steps up, has his Derringer in hand and is trading shots—him only firing his two barrels—with the four bandits at the rear of the coach.

Bringing the now dead bandit's shotgun up, I cut loose at the nearest of the bandits, at the rear of the Concord and at no more than twenty paces, and blow a leg out from under him. I'm on my belly, using the body of the dead bandit as cover. At least two slugs slam into the dead man's body.

Slade is down, but the trapper is back inside the Coach and has his French revolver in hand. He's moved to the far side and is shooting away. I glance up to see Alabama flat on top the baggage on top the coach and he's firing as well.

Both ladies are hotfooting it down the road, holding their skirts up, and heading for the Transcontinental or whatever is that direction.

It turns out the two riflemen back in the rocks was a lie, either that or they hightailed it when the shooting started. Two of the bandits at the rear of the coach are on the ground, one kicking, the other not moving. The one kicking is only kicking with one leg as I've blown his other half off. It's bleeding like a fire hose, and when it stops spurting, he stops kicking or even twitching.

The other two bandits are scrambling out over the rocks with old trapper Porter Polkinghorn hotfooting it after them firing his French revolver every dozen leaps or so.

I clamor to my feet and find Slade on his knees holding a hole in his gut, and coughing up blood. I hurry to the other side of the coach and discover Sandy, the driver, on his face, a hand over a hole clean though his throat. A lot of blood is soaking into the black rock road. And as I reach to try and stem his bleeding, he stops blowing bubbles out of the hole in his neck, and, eyes open and staring at the sky as if hopefully seeing a stairway to heaven, stills. Alabama has climbed down, is kneeling by his friend and looks up and clamps his jaw and shakes his head sadly. The bandit, who stopped us like a stranded traveler is, as Alabama warned, nearly cut in half. A chunk the size of his head is blown out of his side and lung and intestine hangs there. He won't be robbing any more. His jaw is slack and his eyes dead and staring.

The women have stopped a hundred yards down the road and I wave them back. They hesitate, but finally start walking our way. I return to Slade and find him now sunk to his back, talking through clinched teeth. Blood seeps from the corner of his mouth.

He manages, "Tasting ... blood. Bad ... right?"

"Right," I say, and place a hand on his shoulder. "You likely saved lots of folks, Mr. Slade."

"Got a brother in Washoe Meadows and ... and a deed and belongings in that leather satchel ... atop the coach. If'n I don't make it, you'll get them to him?" I take Slade for a hard man, but his eyes are pleading. He reaches to his four-in-hand tie and pulls his diamond stick pin free and hands it to me. "Take this, for you, and swear."

It's the opposite direction from where I'm heading, but the man backed my play and it looks as if he's going to die for the effort. So, stick pin or no stick pin, I nod, "I will."

"Swear?"

"I swear. I do swear, Slade."

"It's not Slade, it's Flannigan. Bother ... damn, that hurts."

"Brother?" I press as he's fading. "Not Slade?"

"Times is it's best not to advertise your name. Shriver Flannigan ... nickname is Shivers." He coughs and sputters a minute, having trouble speaking. "Whiskey?" he says, eyes pleading even more.

"Whiskey," I yell at the others, and to my surprise, Mrs. Sniddleman reaches in the reticula she's clung to on her attempted escape, pulls out a little medicine bottle and hands it to me.

"Ain't medicine," she says, looking a little sheepish.

I hand it to Slade ... Flannigan. "Hold my head up," he says. I plop on my butt and prop his head up on my thigh. He spits blood, then takes a long draw on the bottle, wheezes, coughs and stops breathing.

"I believe Mr. Slade has passed. God bless him," Mary Ann Merriweather says, bending over.

Alabama is near, and rather coldly says, "Mr. Jackson,

you and Mr. Polkinghorn will have a reward coming when we reach the station at Fort Hall."

"Mr. Slade deserves a share or his family does," I say.

"You know his family?" Alabama asks.

"He made me swear to get his valise ... satchel ... to his brother at Washoe Meadows."

"Then his brother can pick up his share at the Reno Station."

"Fair enough," I say.

"Load that luggage that's in the boot up on top and pile Mr. Sandy and Mr. Slade in its place."

"And those others," I say, referring to the bandits, three of who are dead in the road and one still kicking, but less every minute.

"I'll report it at Fort Hall. Should they want to send a burial detail out, so be it. But they done killed my friend Sandy, so if the beetles and buzzards make dung outta 'em, so be it."

I shrug, expecting some argument from the ladies, but almost in unison they say, "So be it."

And in a half hour, after Alabama has checked the busted spoke and determined the wheel sound enough to reach Fort Hall, we're on the road again with Alabama driving and Polkinghorn riding shotgun. Me? I have the not-so-tough duty of guarding the ladies in the coach.

Damned if I'm not heading for Washoe Meadows and the Reno stage stop, only twenty-five miles from Virginia City, Nevada, and, with luck, a reunion with my friend Jasper Todd Jefferson.

And riding there with one of the most beautiful young women I've ever met.

The Lord works in mysterious ways.

CHAPTER 18

CAMPED NEAR FORT HALL IS A LARGE CIRCLE OF WAGONS, even since the wedding of both sides of the country by the Transcontinental Railroad, folks have continued to train-up wagons to cross the country—particularly if bound to Washington or Oregon. Nearer the Snake River is another large camp, only this one made up of animal skin teepees, not canvas-covered wagons.

The stage station is not far from the fort's gate. The station agent, a stout fellow name of Jenkins, immediately opens and counts the contents of the strong box and finds almost eighteen pounds of fine gold dust, over six thousand dollars in paper money, and eight hundred in coin. He has to weigh and repackage the dust, verifying the weight, but soon announces the value of the Wells Fargo Overland Stage cargo at eleven thousand four hundred dollars. The reward at ten percent is consequently eleven hundred forty dollars, split three ways is three hundred eighty dollars each.

He questions me as to Mr. Slade's—Flannigan's—relative in Washoe Meadows and after paying Mr. Polkinghorn and myself, says he'll wire the station master in Washoe with instructions to pay the proper amount to a Mr. Shriver Flannigan, when I present him to collect. And that he can expect me to deliver a valise and some personal belongings to Shriver.

The ladies are provided fine quarters in the fort. As I'm a little stained with the blood of the bandit I used as cover and maybe a touch of Flannigan's, and soiled from rolling on the black rock road, I find a fort laundress and change into my rough clothes while she cleans and presses my suit, white muslin shirt, and four-in-hand tie.

We say goodbye to Alabama here, as he'll be driving another Concord back to Virginia City, and meet Trevor Tull, our driver, and Cordell McAllister, our shotgun guard, for the trip on to Ogden and the railroad connection.

More and more as we bounce and sway our way to Ogden, I'm infatuated with Miss Mary Ann Merriweather. And angry with myself and my personal history, as I'm compelled to create a tale about my past. I doubt if she'd be impressed with a mother who died of the pox after a sordid, if not chosen, life as a pleasure lady. And with a father who was a hardscrabble miner and died a drunk. And, of course, my own dubious history of seven years in one of the roughest prisons west of the Mississippi. But, as much as I hate lying to a woman to whom I'm so attracted, I can't relate the truth of my past to her as I'm still a wanted man. Posters bearing my likeness still adorn post offices, express offices, and stations even this far south.

So, I remain reticent to talk about myself, for good reason.

Our trip to Ogden is uneventful after leaving Fort Hall, with only two more layovers and a hard, long last day. I'm able to offer my services to Miss Mary Ann Merriweather transporting her small steamer trunk from the stage station across the street to a Lady Anne's, a lady's boarding house, then again this morning to the train station where, as she's travelling first class, she'll enjoy the luxury of a small cabin with two berths that she's sharing with an older woman I've yet to meet. As far as I can see, the only two ladies on the train.

Myself? I'm relegated to third class, a hard bench seat two cars distant. I am pleased and encouraged, that she's agreed to meet me for the noon meal in the dining car, which separates my not so elegant facility from hers.

The train arrives at 10:22, only an hour late, and takes on water, wood, and supplies for the dining car kitchen. In addition to the steam engine and wood car, is a dining car, five passenger cars, and three freight cars—one of which is marked U.S. Mail in big white letters. Two stock cars follow, filled—I can tell by the nervous neighing, nickering and occasional hoof striking the plank walls— with horses. Bringing up the rear is a caboose. Up front, the engine is manned by an engineer and fireman, then we have four conductors, a cook and two waiters, and I have no idea who or how many man the mail car.

We are on the rails for little more than an hour when I realize it's noon and move back through the following second class car to the dining car. I'm surprised to be met by a waiter who asks to see my ticket, then informs me I'm not entitled, as a third-class passenger, to enter the dining car. I'm expected to eat at the various stops along the way, or carry on my own grub. I explain to him I have an appointment with a first-class passenger and he's adamant that I cannot enter. Tempted as I am to relieve him of his front teeth, I clamp my jaw and wait just outside the dining car door, which has a glass-paneled door, until I see Mary Ann enter and be escorted to a table.

I waste no time striding to her side and am in the process of informing her of my lack of welcome, when the officious bug-eyed waiter runs up and pokes me in the chest with a finger and yells, "Out, out, I told you ...."

That's as far as he gets before I grasp the finger and give it a twist. He goes to his knees and turns white in the face.

"Mr. Jackson!" Mary Ann snaps.

I release him, shaking my head, and apologize to her. "I'm sorry Mary Ann, but I can't abide a rude man."

I tip my hat to her, spin on a heel and head back my way.

I'm only back on my hard bench for a few minutes, and, just about the time the heat in my backbone resides, three conductors, followed by the sputtering waiter, arrive. The largest of the three demands to see my ticket.

"You're third class and not allowed in the dining car," he says, glowering at me.

"Now I know," I say, and turn to watch the country roll by.

"You'll be put off at the next station as you've assaulted our employee ...."

"I paid my fare," I say, rising to my feet, my hand resting on the Colt at my side.

"Don't matter. We'll refund the balance due you, but you're off the train."

The heat is back on my backbone. "Sir, I mean no offense to any who treat me with the respect any man is due. This wart," I point at the waiter, "poked me in the chest and was rude as a rutting hog. No man treats me like that."

The big conductor turns to the waiter and demands, "Did you put a hand on this passenger?"

"I may have touched him," he stammers, "but he grabbed my finger and damn near broke ...."

"I was hoping it was busted," I say.

The conductor turns back to me. "Don't go to the dining car again, then turns back to the waiter, "And don't you ever lay a hand on a passenger or I'll break your damn arm, not just a finger." He turns back to me, "We square here?"

I extend my hand, he takes it, and we shake. "I'm Brad Jackson," I offer, nearly making an error and telling him my real name.

"Reggie Smithson, head conductor."

"Nice to make your acquaintance, Mr. Smithson, and to meet a fair and just gentleman."

"Enjoy the trip," he says, and they all leave.

It's no more than an hour before I look up and Miss Mary Ann is standing near. She gives me a tight smile, and offers, "He had no reason to poke you and be insulting," she says.

"Actually, he had told me earlier I was not allowed in the dining car, but I told you I'd meet you and the devil himself couldn't keep me from explaining ...."

"I thought about it and understand. We have a stop to take on water and wood in Nemesis and maybe we could enjoy a cup of tea at the station."

"I'd like that," I say. We trade smiles, and she heads back to the high-class end of the train.

Then the train's brakes squeal and she's thrown forward, about to go to her back in the aisle. I leap to my feet and am able to catch her under the arms, brace us both, and as the train slows get her back to her feet.

"You all right?" I ask.

"Thank God you were there," she says, but I'm more concerned with the reason for the sudden stop, reach into the overhead and grab my Winchester.

"Maybe you better find your cabin?" I say over my shoulder as I move forward. I don't bother to see if she leaves but head to the engine end of the car and peer out the door as the train stills.

On a ridge no more than a half mile south of the tracks, I spot more than two dozen mounted Indians, then realize what they seem to be enjoying. At least two sections of rail have been removed from the bed and cast aside. Had we not been making a slight upgrade and slowed by the climb, we'd likely have crashed and piled the cars up like blowdown timber.

As it is, we came to a stop only a car length from the sabotage.

And in sight of a war party.

CHAPTER 19

A HALF-DOZEN OTHER MEN APPEAR AT TRAIN SIDE, AND I climb down and join them as we move forward. I glance back. At least two dozen gun barrels appear out train windows.

As we inspect the damage, with one eye turned toward the savages, I see them wheel their horses and disappear behind the ridge.

The engineer yells to us. "An express train is due here in forty minutes. We've got to get this track relayed and get switched to a spur."

The conductors have appeared at our side and have a bucket of spikes, and a half dozen sledgehammers and pry bars in hand.

The engineer has become a construction boss and the head conductor, Smithson, his foreman.

The engineer yells and me and a couple of other fellas who are carrying Winchesters and Sharps, "You three move on out four or five car lengths, a hundred paces, and stand guard. I'll give two quick toots on the whistle when we're ready to haul out ... damn savages," then he yells to his crew of a dozen men. "Move it a'fore we get an express train up our butt."

The Indians seemed amused to watch from a distance and don't return to challenge what's likely four dozen guns. The makeshift crew quickly has the track in place, the whistle toots twice, we run for our cars, and the train begins to chug forward before I can reach my seat.

Miss Mary Ann Merriweather is nowhere in sight, and I elect not to try and pass through the dining car to see if she's ensconced in her cabin. I've had enough conductor trouble.

It's a nice sunny day, which I'd normally relish, but the fact is with ash from the steam engine continually blowing in the windows, and it's too warm to close them, I've been more comfortable. My rolled-up duster serves as a pillow and I'm about to doze off, when someone parks beside me on the hard-wooden seat.

And it's a very pleasant someone. Mary Ann. With a mug in hand.

"Were you napping?" she asks.

"Resting my eyes. As much as I welcome your company, you'd be better off back aways. We get lots of ash."

She digs in her reticula, comes out with a roll surrounding a slice of ham and a bottle of beer and hands it over. "If Mohammad can't come to the mountain then the mountain will come to him," she says and laughs with a tinkle I've come to welcome.

"That's just too dang thoughtful. I'm obliged."

"Least I could do for a soul who'd stand out in the wilds between me and a band of savages."

It's my turn to laugh. Then I ask, "Can I share with you?"

"I've eaten my fill, thank you."

"So, this teaching job you're taking. What's it all about?"

"A lady's finishing school. It was founded as the Young Ladies Seminary in Benicia, north of Oakland, has recently moved to Oakland and is the first women's college in the west. It's soon to be renamed Mill's College."

"You are much younger than I am. How is it you can teach at a college?"

She laughs that tinkle again. "I'm twenty-two, not that a lady should divulge her age. I was fortunate to attend Mount Holyoke women's college in South Hadley, Massachusetts, and will teach the classics."

"The classics?" I ask, a little embarrassed about being so damn ignorant.

"Greek and Roman history and literature."

I'm silent for a moment, then can't help but ask, "Dang if I can figure how that will help folks get along in the world."

She laughs again. "It's said if you don't know the mistakes folks have made in history, then man is destined to repeat them. So, I must believe, history is very important."

I stare out the window for a moment, then wonder how important my own history has been, and if folks could learn anything from it. I guess they could learn lots of things not to do. Then I realize I have learned lots of things not to do again. Maybe that's important as well.

We ride along in silence for a while as I finish my

sandwich. I'm sad to say I think this woman is way too smart for me. And I'm sure with her accomplishments as one of the few women in the country who's graduated from a college, she would be even less impressed than most that my only term in an institution ended with me escaping, not graduating.

In my fancy duds, I know I look like something I'm not. It's often said you can put a red ribbon bow on a hound's neck, but he's still a hound.

I decide then and there that for both our sakes I will stay away from Miss Mary Ann. That's doing her the biggest favor I can think of.

As I'm silent for a long time, she finally says she's tired and believes she'll retire to her cabin for a nap. I thank her again for the snack, and we part. Likely for the last time.

I again roll up my duster to use as a pillow, lean against the window mullion and let the rocking lull me to sleep.

Not knowing how long I've slept, I'm awakened by the train squeaking and rattling to a stop. Rubbing my eyes, I see a water tank with a long spigot being lowered to refill the steam engines tank and two fellows nearby at the entrance to a covered but open-sided building filled with firewood. As soon as the train stills, they begin tossing wood from one to the other then up to a catcher on the wood car.

I yawn and stretch wide, then hear the report of a rifle. I look back to see four riders on my side of the train, back near the first-class cars, all mounted and waving a variety of firearms and yelling at folks on the train. I turn back, and the fellows tossing wood have palmed revolvers and are waving the engineer and fireman off the train.

From what I can see of them, they're a motley bunch, ragged, dirty, but well-armed.

My worldly goods are in my carpetbag under my seat along with those of my departed friend, Flannigan. My Winchester is in the overhead and my Colt on my hip. I guess what the Indians couldn't do, some gang of hooligans is going to try and accomplish—and very likely accomplish over my dead body.

But if history has taught me anything, it's that a fellow has to take care of himself and his own. That, and the fact you can't take care of anyone else if you don't take care of yourself.

And 'anyone else' at the moment, is Miss Mary Ann Merriweather. I look back toward the first-class cars and these renegades are dragging folks off the train and searching them. One big filthy galoot is running his hands all over Mary Ann. She's screaming and he's laughing like Beelzebub is encouraging him. The heat rattles my backbone and my mouth goes dry as I clamp my jaw.

There must be more of them on the other side of the train, and I yell at a rough looking fellow across the car from me. "How many on your side?"

"There're five empty horses tied off aways, but they must be aboard."

I look off into the distance and see four horses tied to some mesquite, then back to the woodshed and see the legs of more than one fellow sticking out behind. I'd guess they are the train company roustabouts either knocked cold, dead, or hogtied.

I've got my Winchester in hand and see at least four other fellows are armed and looking like they are as unwilling to give up their goods as am I.

"All y'all throw down your iron," a voice rings out from the door at the rear of our car.

One of the other men yells back. "Why don't you stick your ugly mug in here and come get 'em?"

It seems the fellow who's wanting our weapons doesn't care about what condition our weapons might be in, or us for that matter, as a stick of dynamite, fuse smoking, sails down the aisle, bouncing along as merrily as can be.

CHAPTER 20

IT'S MOVE, OR WAIT TO MOVE IN VARIOUS DIRECTIONS IN various pieces.

I'm sure the hooligan who tossed the killer stick figured all would run the opposite direction. Times is the only way to survive is to do what's not expected, so I run toward the fella that chucked the killer stick at us, who's wisely ducked back out of the way of the explosion and out of sight. His mistake.

With my Colt palmed in my right and my Winchester in my left, I charge through the door and he's on my left, so I fill his gut with an ounce of lead as I pass. The old boy looks very surprised as he's blown out over the landing rail onto the ground some five feet below.

Hell, I'm on a roll, so I keep running. The second-class car seems of more interest to the robbers and there's two of them, busily collecting valuables from the twenty or so passengers. I duck in between the seats for cover as they both spin my way; my Colt roaring is quickly overshadowed by the explosion I've left behind. The one closest to me I've gut shot as I dove for cover and he's on a knee when the blast, more powerful down the center aisle, blows him over backward into his fellow train robber. I'm on my feet as number two is trying to regain his. He's head down bent double and my second shot takes him in the backbone just below the neck, and he drops on top of his gut-shot pardner. I keep moving and give the first gut-shot hombre another in the back of the head as I pass over them.

But there's another coming my way out of the dining car and he's firing as he comes. I spin to the side, hit in the thigh, but just a flesh wound, and drop my Winchester clattering on the floor as I fall between the seats and flop out into the aisle with my upper body. I guess he thinks I'm out of the game as he keeps coming with his revolver swinging at his side.

I fan two at him, only ten feet from me, and his mouth drops open as he's flung backward flat on his back. He's still flopping around, his firearm lost under the seats. I grab up my Winchester as I'm down to one load in the Colt and think trying to reload would be unwise. I'm hearing shots fired both ahead and behind me, and hope one of the lowlifes is not leveling on my spine from behind.

The dining car is empty, except for that smart-ass waiter I traded words with before I bent his finger crooked, and he won't be rude ever again. He's on his face in the aisle with lung blood bubbling out his back about heart high.

So, I keep going, but am rocked before I enter the first-class car—another much larger explosion—where the aisle turns to the side of the car and cabins line the other. No one in that aisle, and I dare to stick my head out a window and see robbers running for the hole where the door to the mail car was before being blown to splinters.

I could care less about somebody's postcards or even the gold and paper money I'm sure they carry. I'm looking for Miss Mary Ann, but she's nowhere in sight. Five hooligans are passing white sacks out of the mail car and stuffing them in saddlebags, but I'm seen as I try to get the barrel of my rifle out the window and barely hit the floor after a shot shatters the mullion, when a dozen quickly fired shots blow the closed windows on either side all to hell—the first-class cabin has window glass.

I scamper on my hands and knees, below window height, back the way I've come, into the second-class car, before I try the window again with my Winchester. I only get off one shot and miss that, when again gunshots splatter wood all around and I have to dive for cover.

I move another five seats back toward my car, and this time only peek out the window to see if I can spot Miss Mary Ann and the ugly renegade who was manhandling her.

But I can't see much of him, surely not enough for a target, as he's got her on the back of his horse and is galloping away.

My blood runs cold thinking of her fate, stolen away by a renegade bunch, some of whom look to be half-breeds.

Her head is slumped to the side and I fear she's knocked silly or unconscious. I get back in position and even though I can't get a shot at him, I do take a shot at one of his partners, who's among the half dozen riding away. There's another woman on the back of another robber's horse, so I pick the one nearest at the back of the pack and miss him, but my shot is obviously low at the hundred yard or more distance. His horse only takes four or five more leaps then goes head over heels, dumping his rider who hits hard enough to knock him loop-legged and his hat, with an extra wide brim, flying. He's on his butt and sitting up, which gives me lots of time to make my next shot count. He jerks, bends forward and doesn't twitch again. The horse is on its side, kicking, but not able to rise.

And I don't know if it was even my shot that did the deed as others are firing. I hear shots from the last car, the caboose, and from the third-class cars in the front.

It seems these owlhoots made a drastic error picking a train full of competent shooters.

I move to the far side of the car and gaze out to see if there are any more targets, and see none. But I see something better. A fine palomino horse is standing, grazing, dragging his reins in slow steps as if he hadn't just been in the middle of a small war.

I head to the end of the car and move down and casually walk his way. He shies a bit but I step on his reins, and that stops him. He must belong to one of the dead robbers. I mount up and ride to the engine and see both engineer and fireman hit. The engineer is on his face, unmoving, and the fireman is on his butt holding his stomach with both hands.

I round the engine, remember the legs I saw at the rear of the wood building and ride there. I see two men tied and struggling with their bonds. I have a folding knife, dismount and cut them loose.

"Is they gone?" one of them asks.

"Yes, and took a couple of ladies with them," I say, in more of a growl than an even voice.

He points up the hill aways where there's a clapboard cabin, "I got a key up yonder and need to wire ahead. They'll send the law and meet the train down the rail."

"If the train is going anywhere. Looks like the engineer is shot dead and the fireman wounded badly. Unless the conductor ...."

"He can't," the fellow says.

"I'm going back to my seat and getting some things then I'm trailing this bunch. You tell the law I'm out there when and if they get here."

"Will do. What the hell are you gonna do against a half dozen or more hard men?"

"I'll know that when I catch up with them."

I mount up and gig the horse to my train car, tie him to the handrail, and am pleased to find my carpetbag still in place under my seat, what's left of it. The bag is scarred and scorched, but whole. The head conductor, Reggie Smithson, is helping some others tend to those wounded by the explosion. I jump down to the palomino, who has a set of generous saddle bags, and they're not full. I have one box of .44/.40 that will fit both Colt and Winchester. There's a sack of jerky and one of hardtack in the bags, as well as a decent hunting knife with an eight-inch blade in scabbard, a tin pan and cup, and a pair of water bags, one hanging each side of the horn. I pack my necessaries and valuables from carpetbag to saddlebags.

This robber must have been a cowhand at one time or another, and maybe a vaquero—his hat is as big as a sombrero—as there's a fine woven leather reata hanging from a saddle tie. I replace a rolled blanket tied behind the saddle with my duster. Rolled in the duster is a coach gun I've picked up next to the body of a robber, and I change from my brogans and good suit back into my boots and rough clothes. My valuables go deep into the saddle bags, but I guess it doesn't matter as I'm likely to be far too dead to enjoy my riches.

I'd guess I'm about to be a one-man posse.

CHAPTER 21

REGGIE HAS RELIEVED THE DEAD ROBBERS OF A FINE MODEL 3 American Smith and Wesson—also in .44/.40—and I take possession of it and a coach gun, but only have one live shell of the two in the chambers, and four more that were in its former owner's pockets. He won't be needing them.

I ask Reggie to leave my beat-up carpetbag and contents with the station at Washoe Meadows, and he agrees to do so.

"Tell you truthful, Mr. Jackson," he says after I hand him my valise, "I got to think you're a damn fool going after them filthy fellas alone. Wait until the law ..."

"Hell, they could be halfway to Mexico before the law shows up."

"They'll be headed this way behind another engine, soon as they get word and get moving."

"And dark will be on us and they can't track in the dark. I'm moving out. If I don't show back up, there are belongings, including a letter, in that bag for a Shivers Flannigan. See he gets them should I not show up in a fortnight. His brother died alongside me while fighting off some other robbers ...."

"You ain't had the best of luck," Reggie says, with a hard smile.

"I'm here, they ain't, so I'm feeling pretty damn fortunate."

I'm thinking prison was more peaceful than stagecoach or train travel but don't say it. I'm now the killer of five men—that worthless sheriff and four or more robbers. I guess I should be feeling lots of remorse, but dang if I don't think, had I not been the lucky one, I'd be worm food, not them. That tempers my resolve and remorse is no longer considered.

I gig the horse, pass the last robber I shot and see his horse is still twitching. I guess one more shot won't be too much of a waste. I dismount and put him out of his hurt with one to the head. While I'm down, I gather up the robber's wide-brimmed distinctive hat that has a wide bright orange hat band. I gather it up for two reasons: one, this sun, even in May, can be blistering; and two, I'm on a robber's horse and wearing one's distinctive hat, so I'm less likely to be ambushed should the robber band detect a man dogging their trail. They'll likely think I'm their compatriot.

At least it sounds good when you conjure it.

I'm pleased the palomino doesn't go crazy hearing a shot so near and only flinches and side steps a little.

My leg, with a good groove along the outer side of my thigh, is beginning to pain me, so modesty be damned, I drop my pants and tie my bandana around it after stuffing the half-inch-deep gouge with grass. It's not doctor-good as dressings go, but it'll have to do.

"Good horse, Pal," I say, as I mount, then gig him into a fast walk. And I add, "Okay, old buddy, that's your name now, Pal."

There's no sense in pushing him too hard. This high dry desert is not easy on man nor beast, so steady is the plan. I figure my water bag is good for me for three days, but that's without watering Pal, and he'll have to have water as well.

As we top the first rise, riding due south, ninety degrees from the train track, I'm happy to see dark clouds to the southwest coming over some high mountains over that way. They are maybe fifty or more miles away, so I don't expect to cross any fresh water streams coming off their still snow covered tops. With luck we'll have some rain, both to keep us in water and to slow the robbers down. And mud will make tracking easier.

My pants are soaked down to the knee from the thigh wound, but it's stopped bleeding and the dressing is holding. It has made me grit my teeth more than once as it reminds me I've been shot. Now I'll be scarred on the leg, belly, and back from the through and though I took in Phillipsburg. I'll win no beauty contest, but then I wouldn't have without a scar.

The good news is a half-dozen, mounted men on shod horses leave a trail a half-blind man could follow.

So, I do, until darkness shuts my pursuit down after maybe ten or twelve miles. I can't help but think of what Miss Mary Ann may be going through as I water Pal with four topped off cups, then I stake him out in a patch of green, gnaw some jerky and hardtack myself and chase it with three or four generous swallows of water. He's at least four times my body weight, maybe five, so I'll have to judge what we both need if we must ration. Blackfeet Pete taught me a man might as well carry a day's ration of water in his belly as in a bag.

I pray those renegades will light far too tired to have their way with Miss Mary Ann, as a refined lady like her might be so shamed she'd do herself in or fight so hard they would do the deed for her.

Tomorrow, half way into the day, should I find water to stoke Pal's thirst, I'll pick up the pace. Leading the way, not having to trail, they have the advantage. They can travel at night. However, they have no reason to think anyone is on their tail—at least no law dogs. So maybe they will not push it too hard.

I awake before sunup having to rid my body of the little water I took and, when done, shake my head and cuss myself. What kind of fool am I, off into a damn desert I know little or nothing about, riding down a half dozen hard men who'd think nothing of leaving my bones to bleach in the desert sun, after a women I've known for only a few days and to whom I owe nothing more than a sandwich and a bottle of flat beer.

I take the time to unwrap the bandana on my thigh and clean as much grass from the wound as feels wise, much is stuck in scab and removing it would only start the bleeding again. I can only imagine I'll need every drop of blood in the ol' body if I come up against six or more hooligans.

The good news is we get a rain in the night, not terribly hard, not enough to make the ravines run, but enough to leave some puddles where the desert floor is hard enough to hold it. I'm able to let Pal have his fill and to fill my one water bag that was a third empty. I'm tempted to not fill it with the brackish water I can get from puddles, but then figure a little mud won't hurt me.

As we start out again, I gig Pal into a quick walk, then see we have a fairly steep rise ahead—a hill at least five hundred feet high. I switchback up to the highest spot with the hopes of being able to scan the country for some distance ahead. Although much of what I can see is occluded by thickening patches of tall greasewood and scattered white pine.

He's puffing and sucking wind by the time we reach the top, so I dismount and let him graze and blow while I perch my butt on a cairn of rocks—likely a marker placed by some tribe of Indians—and shade my eyes from the sun rising on my right. As I hoped, it's an excellent perch, and I'm not there more than ten minutes before I see riders sky-lined two hills south of me, crossing a rise some lower than my perch. I cannot tell—it's more than a mile, maybe two—if any of them are riding double. But pray they are.

I put him into a canter on the downhill slope, let him walk up, and canter down again. I've gained some advantage with last night's rain. Six horses have made a highway of tracks in the muddy soil and I can track at a gallop, maybe even by moonlight, as no matter if the mud dries, they've left deep tracks weaving around rabbit brush and the occasional manzanita.

Never having cowboy'd or not having a daddy who owned a ranch, I'm not much of a plainsman, but do know the occasional shrub or tree. And Blackfeet Pete Stealshorse, who was my cellmate, taught me lots by drawing and telling me colors of blooms and such. I know those I've mentioned and the slopes of mountain mahogany, buckwheat, and bitterbrush we're riding into. The bad news is the low brush is becoming so thick it's blocking my view of track, but the good news is it's allowing them to ride a straight trail as there's nothing tall enough to have to avoid. The country is more broken now, with some deep ravines, some rock shelves, and a table rock mountain not far ahead.

I'm wondering if I'm gaining on them, maybe too fast in the light, when I rein up to see a deep hoof print. It's slowly filling with seeping water.

They must be just ahead.

CHAPTER 22

I GLANCE TO MY RIGHT, TO THE WEST, AND SEE THE SUN IS about to touch the mountain tops in the distance.

Dismounting, I let Pal graze and I limp up the low rise ahead of me, moving even more slowly, cautiously, as I near the top. Limping as my leg is paining me. I'm getting a niggle on the back of my neck like I'm walking into something, so hunker down and move even more slowly.

No more than three-eighths of a mile ahead, the renegades are entering a cut, following a dry creek bed. The table rock mountain with steep granite sides is no more than one quarter of a mile ahead of them. They are headed straight for it.

I'm wondering if they have a permanent camp there? If so, I'm sure they'll have a guard posted somewhere overlooking their back trail. Any cautious man would. Any man expecting a posse hunting him sure as hell would.

I keep my spot, low in the brush, until they disappear into the cut, then retrieve Pal. I know where they've gone, so I have no need of tracking. And if they have a guard, he'll be watching their back trail expecting a tracker leading a posse.

I'm smiling, if a tight grimace of one. As I'm sure two of them have riders behind—both the women, I presume.

So, as I think I know their destination, I'm not following their trail. I mount up and head due east, staying behind the low rise between me and the stream-cut ravine until I figure I've covered at least a half mile, then I turn south again. The cut they've followed is the simple way through a rugged brush-covered hill but appears to end at the base of the table mountain in a rock escarpment. Near the box canyon's narrow entrance, I'm facing a steep bluff some forty or fifty feet high, but I can make out game trails going up the steep side to the ridge. I've seen mule deer in the distance and a few antelope, and I imagine this is a trail followed by muleys. If a muley can make it, I can do so on horseback, or at worst will have to dismount and lead Pal up.

But I don't have to lead, I'm able to ride to the top and see a gentle rise no more than a half mile to the base of the table rock. The cut they followed is west of me. It looks to me like the trail they took has to end in a box canyon surrounded by the steep sides of the table mountain. But I can't be sure. There could be a way out and maybe they will continue up to the top of the mountain through some cut or cave or out of the canyon another way, which means it's not truly a box canyon. I can't imagine that someone being pursued would purposely trap themselves.

As much as I'd like to ride into their camp with guns blazing—if this is their camp—it would be suicide, and I won't be able to save Mary Ann if I'm coyote chow. I find a shallow ravine leading away from a trickle of a spring at the base of the cliff-sided table mountain, a ravine lushly lined with grass. I stake out Pal and start making my way along the base of the escarpment. I note the sun is below the mountain tops to the west; the sky is now streaked with yellow and gold and the edge of clouds as brilliant as the double eagles in my saddlebags. I likely have less than a half hour of decent light. But that's not so bad. If this is their home camp, they'll have a cabin with oil lamps or maybe a campfire, if not more than one. I should easily be able to see them before they see me.

However, what I see is a guard stationed atop rough rocks flanking the ravine they entered. So, this is their camp, at least for tonight. I'd have missed him had he not had a small fire, maybe to heat his supper or just to keep warm. In the failing light, I can make out the game trail up to his location from the box canyon.

He doesn't see me, as I'm higher than he is, and he's watching their back trail below. It's a good thing I didn't try to approach from the north as he'd have spotted me a half mile distant. As it is, I drop back and do my best to stay out of sight, climbing all the time. I reach the table top, continue south until I come to the edge of the box canyon and discover I was right about it. A hundred feet below, in the forty acres of box canyon, there are two cabins, rough limb and brush corrals holding at least two dozen horses and a three-sided barn—just little more than a shed—in the bottom. And it's easy to see why they picked this as a permanent camp site as there's a half-acre pond. Ponds come dear in this desert. I noticed some scrubby pines atop the table mountain and it seems there may be a few in the box canyon. I can't see another exit but am sure there is one and might spot one in the light of day. It's now getting too damn dark. I'd like to make my way down to the canyon floor and put the sneak on the cabins, but the cliff side would be dangerous to try and traverse in darkness, or even in daylight. And again, I can do the women no good if I'm a pile of coyote crap.

The number of horses makes me wonder how many occupy this camp. A half dozen rode in, one of whom, I imagine, is standing guard. Or maybe he has been there guarding the entrance since they rode out to rob the train.

I know there are six hooligans in the camp, but there could as easily be sixteen. The cabins are large enough to hold that many bunks.

The hell of it is there won't be a better time to move on the camp. Letting them rest up from a gunfight, losing a good number of their gang and from riding hard for many hours, will only make them more dangerous.

Fact is I'm hoping they're celebrating, having gotten away with whatever they stole from that mail car—and generally it would be plenty. I hope they're busy. I can't imagine them bemoaning the loss of a few of their fellow hooligans as the share will be that much larger for each survivor. I don't imagine these are the type of folks to mourn their dead.

And celebrating among the like of them surely means a few jugs of corn or pulque to pass around—and the partaking of women. That sends a chill down my back. The other alternative is they hope to ransom Mary Ann and the other lady, whoever she may be, and will offer them unharmed, including molestation, with the threat of the alternative. I can only hope.

No matter, the time to strike is while the iron is hot and they will have little or no idea someone is already onto their location. They'll be figuring it will be a day or two before they're tracked, if ever.

So, I backtrack, having to be extra careful descending the rock face down to where I have Pal staked. My dang leg is driving me a little crazy, I keep checking to see if it's bleeding again, but so far so good.

Since I can't descend the rock face inside the box canyon, I decide to try subterfuge and have high hopes the last thing or person they'll suspect is one riding right in as if he shared ownership. I'm proud of myself for picking up the hat, worn by the robber who rode Pal. But I'm going to let the moon rise—it's just now on the eastern horizon—until I know it's well after midnight before I make my play.

The wind is picking up, and that's helpful as the sound of pines bending and sage and greasewood rattling hides that of hoof beats and the creak of saddle leather.

I gig Pal back the way we came in, out of sight of the guard, then turn him west until I figure I'm on the well beaten trail they made. I'm hoping we get some rain again as the guard will be less likely to see me at a distance, but it's not to be even though clouds occasionally occlude the moon.

With the moon directly overhead, I say a short prayer, hope He listens to a fella who's killed more than a handful of His creations and urge Pal into a slow walk. I want to appear to be a wounded or at least very exhausted rider, returning home after being separated from his *amigos*.

As I near the cut, the dry streambed, and the rock face

with the guard atop, I can't help but gaze up to see if the guard is drawing a bead on me, but he's nowhere to be seen. And even when the canyon widens, I see no one. I was praying I wouldn't have to trade shots with the guard. That would alert those in the camp, and my only choice would be to backtrack like the hounds of hell were snapping at my heels, which would likely be happening.

Just inside the mouth of the forty-acre box canyon, I dismount and tie Pal to a small pine, which I'm a little surprised to see in this desert. I guess I've been gently climbing since leaving the rails.

I'm pleased to see there are no lights in the windows of either cabin.

I put the sneak on the nearest one and damn near stumble over an outlaw who's on his butt leaning against a makeshift corral fence post, hat pulled low over his eyes. And, I note while pulling my Colt, he's snoring as loud as a horse snorting. I can smell his kerosene breath and the booze on it from four feet away—dang near wilts my eyelashes. But just to be extra cautious, I flip the Colt and grab it by the barrel. I knock his hat off with one hand and smack him a good one on the pate. He oofs and sags to the ground.

But someone has heard, as a nearby voice calls out, "Who's there?"

CHAPTER 23

I'M DISCOVERED, BUT IT'S A FEMALE VOICE—DEEPER THAN Mary Ann's, but female. I stare into the darkness and make out the form of a woman in skirts who is also seated and leaning against a fence post, the next in line.

"Quiet," I say, having no idea who she is. So, I move her way and realize she's tied, not only leaning but bound to the post.

"You from the train?" I say in as low a voice as I can and still think she'll hear.

"Yes, who ...."

"I'm a friend of Miss Mary Ann's. I followed." She's an older lady, with stringy gray hair, which I'd guess by the quality of her dress, is normally in perfect order. At the moment, she looks like she's been rode hard and put away wet.

"Untie me, please," she asks, keeping her voice low.

I don't oblige her request, rather I pull my folding knife and cut the hemp rope binding her. I ask as I work, "Where's Miss Mary Ann?"

"The smaller cabin. The bastard running this outfit

has her there and has been treating her badly by the sound of things. Thank God they thought my seventy years bony, wrinkled and unattractive."

I help her to her feet. "My horse is tied near the opening. Move quietly. I think there's a guard above in the rocks."

"How did you ...."

"The horse is a palomino, belonging to one of them, as did this hat. I figure in the darkness, he thought I was that fella returning from the robbing or is asleep. If so, let's keep him that way."

"And you?"

"I'm gonna fetch Mary Ann. Don't you be riding out until I get her to you or until you hear lots of gunfire and figure me shot dead."

"Go with God, young man."

"Yes, ma'am," I say, and move away, slipping along the fence line until I have no more cover, then I stand tall and amble to the smaller cabin as if I was just out for a smoke or to relieve myself.

I'm quickly into the moon shadow of the smaller cabin. The only window has shutters but no glass, and I press my ear to the crack between them.

I hear no voices, no snoring, but then hear what sounds like a sob. A woman, sobbing so low to be barely discernible.

Then a voice, "Mr. Scroggins, I have to use the privy."

"Use the damn thunder pot, girl," a gruff voice mumbles.

"I can't not in front ...."

"Hell, I seen all you got," and he laughs a low guffaw.

"Still ...."

"Hell's bells," he says, but I hear him shuffling around, I presume pulling on his boots. Light suddenly streams through the window. He's put match to a lantern.

I position myself behind the door, sorry to note I'm in plain sight of the larger cabin and clearly in the light of the moon.

It's less than a minute before the door opens and Mary Ann, in pantaloons and a chemise, I think they call it, and button shoes only pulled on and not buttoned, steps out. She doesn't notice me. I'm hoping the hooligan she called Mr. Scroggins doesn't either— and he doesn't, as his eyes have yet to adjust to the darkness.

He steps out in long johns, his rear flap flapping, stretches wide, yawns and glances up at the moon, then grunts as I give him the butt of my Colt across his bushy head. He's tougher than the one leaning against the post and only goes to his knees, but the second whack does the job, and he's face down on the ground. It's a bad moon for him, and I hope for the others.

"What ..." Mary Ann mutters, turning back.

I leap the five feet between us and cover her mouth. Her eyes go wide, but she doesn't even try to scream.

"Get dressed ..." I say, whispering in her ear, "... quietly. I'm gonna make sure he stays quiet." When I release her, she crosses her arms in front of her breasts, modestly, even if she's covered by her lace and cotton chemise.

She nods and scampers back into the cabin.

Standing guard, I keep an eye on the first fella I clubbed, the one she's called Scroggins, and on the big cabin. I guess all women take a while dressing, but maybe it's because she's trying to do so in the darkness. It's minutes before she's back out. Now in skirt and blouse.

I whisper to her. "The other lady is at my horse near the opening. I'm going to fetch us a couple more animals. Wait here."

"Kill him," she says, nudging Scroggins with her toe.

I must say I'm surprised, but they say the female of the species is the meanest. I can't help but reply, "Kill him?"

"Yes, kill him."

I shrug. It ain't like I'm a newcomer to the task. So, I bend down and crack him a good one on the noggin. I give her a hard look, "Likely did the job."

"Good," she says. "He's a filthy man and no loss to the world."

There's a dozen lead ropes, but no bridles or saddles on the fence railing next to the gate to the corral holding their animals. I grab two leads and slip inside. I can't see worth a damn, but the first two nearest shy away a time or two, then two others give up, easily approached. I get a rope on the necks and lead them out. Gentle stock I hope, as the women will likely need such. I leave the gate standing wide, praying the animals will decide they want to wander into the desert for some fresh air leaving potential pursuers afoot. I'd stampede them, but that would be noisy.

Then I cuss myself. When I get to where I asked her to wait, Mary Ann's not there.

Damn, I mumble to myself, then only hope against all hope that she's snuck over to find the other lady. As I pass the first owlhoot I whacked, I see he's on his hands and knees, groaning.

I slip over his way, and he looks up as I whack him again, even harder this time, and he goes face first into the mud, or road apples, I hope.

When I lead the animals to where I tied Pal, there's no horse nor any women. Nor my shotgun rolled in my duster. Nor my Winchester in its scabbard. Nor my box of shells or water or grub.

I've long heard that no good deed goes unpunished, and damn if this isn't a good example of that thought.

I slip one of the lead ropes off the smaller of the two animals, tie a Spanish hackamore, and get it on the larger animal. Before I can catch and retie the smaller, he's trotting back to the corral. Damn it. But I don't have the time nor inclination to play catch-a-horse, so I grab a handful of mane, swing up bareback and give heels to the one I have, hoping the ladies are well on their way back to the Transcontinental.

If I don't find them, all this has been for naught. For it's likely these robbers will saddle up and ride down two women in dresses, astraddle a single horse, before sunup.

As I near the open desert end of the creek bed, letting my mount pick his own way, but still wincing as his hooves and iron shoes clatter on the rocks in the dry bed, I'm stopped short by a sharp voice and this one not female.

"Paco, what the hell?"

I look up and, twenty feet above me on a ledge, is the guard, Winchester or Sharps in hand, thinking with the hat I'm wearing that I'm this Paco fella. The muzzle of his long gun is hanging down, so he's not convinced I'm foreign to their rotten bunch.

Mexican, I presume, so I reply, while raising the muzzle of my Colt, "*Hola, amigo.*"

But I'm fooling no one and he sputters, "Who the hell ...."

Then he's blown back against the rock wall as my shot takes him hard in the chest, I hope. He bounces off the wall and somersaults forward, falling and hitting hard on the small boulders next to the stream bed.

I don't wait but pound the animal's ribs with booted heels, and he leaps forward.

The camp is alerted.

But I have to smile as I glance back over my shoulder and see a fair size herd of horses trotting out of the cut behind me. I guess the cold desert air does appeal to them.

CHAPTER 24

As we move at a fast walk, foolish to do otherwise as a horse that breaks a leg in a prairie dog hole won't get a fellow out in front of some angry outlaws.

The moon is still glowing, ducking in and out of clouds, but sinking to the horizon. It won't be long before it's black as a foot up a bull's butt. I can only hope the ladies are moving north. I hope they're moving, but also hope I catch them in the morning light. I have a six shooter on my hip with only five in the spinner, and maybe another ten or twelve in my cartridge belt. A six shooter against a bunch with long arms is bad enough. Running out of cartridges is way worse.

Riding bareback is not my favorite pastime. Thank the good Lord this critter I'm riding seems content to be guided with the hackamore. Had he been a wild one, I'm sure he'd have his way and I'd be arms and legs straight up in a big bitter or sagebrush.

My newly acquired mount is a game one, and strides out even when the underbrush thickens. I'm dozing, my chin on my chest, when my horse neighs and nickers, and I hear a distant neigh in return.

There are plenty of wild horses in this desert, but I glance up and beseech the Lord that it's Pal and the ladies. I rein up and listen, more for some pursuers than in hopes of hearing the women.

My horse neighs again and I do nothing to quiet him. The second neigh that comes from the distance gives me direction. I turn my critter that way and give him my heels.

After a hundred yards, I cup my hands over my mouth and give a yell. "Anybody out there?"

Silence.

"Miss Mary Ann. It's ..." I have to think a second as I'm still not used to being who I've claimed to be. "It's Brad Jackson."

"Brad ... Brad, over here," she shouts back.

I nudge my mount that way and soon see Pal's outline on the top of a small ridge, no more than forty yards away. Slipping off my critter's back, I move forward on foot.

When I'm only ten yards from them, Mary Ann runs forward and throws her arms around me. I enjoy the nearness of her for a moment, then push her back with a hand on both shoulders.

"Y'all ran off and left me."

"That fellow by the fence was up on his hands and knees, and I was frightened. Mrs. Hoolihan said we had to go. Said you told her to go."

"Doesn't matter now. We're back together. What made you pull up?"

"The horse was panting something terrible and we figured we should rest him."

"He's rested now," I say, and pull her over to the bareback nag I've been riding and cup my hands. She gets it and gives me a foot, and I realize she still has on unbuttoned shoes. I guess she's been nowhere near a buttonhook.

I hoist her in the saddle and turn to the lady Mary Ann has called Mrs. Hoolihan. "Ma'am, you mount up and follow. I'm gonna be shank's mare in the lead."

"Shank's mare?" she asks.

"Afoot."

I'm happy to see the ladies safe and darn near as happy to see my weapons, ammunition, water, and grub. Not to speak of the gold nuggets, coins, and paper money I have stashed deep in the bags.

"Let's move out," I say, and am both pleased and displeased to see the sky beginning to lighten in the east. Light means I can see to avoid tripping over a tough sage or in a dog hole, but it also means any pursuers can see us from miles away.

It's full light when I spot a band of riders to the west of us. I drag the ladies from the saddle and lead the horses into some tall sage. Not tall enough, but better than much of the knee-high brush and grass we've been trudging through. I drag my Winchester from the scabbard Pal carries, and hope I don't have to fire on a dozen train robbers. I will, but it will be the end of me should it come to that.

I ask the ladies to keep their heads down, pull a foreleg back on each horse and get them flat on their sides, instructing the ladies to keep weight on their necks to keep them from standing. Then I get high enough to see the riders, judge the distance and get ready to cut loose.

"They have turned south," I report to the ladies. Then I watch and realize that there is a dozen of them. At least half wear the blue of cavalry men, and they're riding side by side as a military detachment would.

"That's a posse and the military," I say.

"Signal them," Mrs. Hoolihan says, stands and let's Pal get to his feet.

I pull my Colt and fire a shot. A quarter mile away, I see them rein up, so I give a two-arm wave like I'm trying to get the train to stop, and I jump up and down as if I was a six-year-old on a school yard. They see me. The column turns our way and comes at a canter.

A man with a generous girth is in the lead, drags his horse to a stop and leaps from it, yelling, "Abigale, Abigale, thank God, Abigale."

Mrs. Hoolihan stumbles through the sage and they embrace.

Mary Ann follows as I walk over to the couple and give a nod to a fella who's now in the lead of the group, obviously, an officer. He gives me a casual salute, but it's the big man hugging the lady, who steps my way and grabs up my hand.

"You must be Jackson. I'm in your debt, Mr. Jackson."

"My pleasure, sir. Mr. Hoolihan, I presume?"

"Actually son, it's Governor Norval Hoolihan."

I want to say, 'the hell you say,' but restrain myself.

"Governor?"

"Yes, son. Governor of Montana Territory, here meeting with the Governor of Nevada." I came up from

Carson City when I heard my wife, on her way to join me, had been absconded with. I don't know how to thank you."

I'm thinking I have a couple of thoughts on the subject—like a pardon—but now is not the time to discuss it. Rather, I extend my hand, "Happy to have been of service, sir." And we shake.

The Governor turns to the Army officer. "My men and I are escorting my wife back to the Transcontinental. I presume you're continuing after the outlaws?"

"We are, sir," the officer answers.

It's time to offer what I know. "If I may, I just came from their hideout. If you'll take a few minutes ...."

He dismounts. "How about coming along?"

"I have business on down the line, but I can give you clear directions." Then I turn back to Governor Hooli-han, as I can see that five others are likely lawmen or a posse, and with the Governor, "Sir, there are likely more than a half-dozen hard men in their camp. I can escort you and the ladies back, but a half-dozen troops could be in great danger riding into this den of snakes." I spend a while describing the hooligans' hideout and the land-marks leading the way, and caution them that the robbers are likely on my trail. I gain a handshake and a thank you from the Captain.

The Governor yells to one of his escorts. "Clevenger, you come with us. The rest of you fellas have my permis-sion to ride on with the Captain, capture those outlaws and return the railroad's money."

The man he called Clevenger turns to the others in civilian clothes, "Y'all are under the command of Captain McNorris, understand?"

They all give him a nod, and he reins over to join us, then gives my thigh a look. "You've been wounded?"

"I have been. A flesh wound. It'll keep until we get the Governor and the ladies back to the rails."

The Governor offers a stirrup to his wife, and she mounts up behind him.

"Then let's be off," Clevenger says, and leads the way. Mary Ann is comfortable on Pal. I'm happy to be out of the clutches of those hooligans and happy to continue to ride bareback, even though my leg continues to remind me it's the host of a deep groove.

It's dark when the oil lamps of the wood and water station lead us into camp. And we're all glad to accept the meager fare of beans and cornbread they offer for a late supper.

The next passenger train is due at 8:30 in the morning, and I'll be privileged to ride the sixteen hours on into Reno with Governor and Mrs. Hoolihan and Miss Mary Ann Merriweather, who, I'm sorry to say, has barely stopped her crying since we arrived at safety.

I wonder, will I ever understand women?

CHAPTER 25

DANG IF THIS ISN'T THE FANCIEST THING I'VE EVER SEEN. The Governor's private train car is parked on a siding as is the nearly destroyed mail car and the stock car which hauled the posse and military here. It will wait for their return, hopefully leading a bevy of prisoners.

As if I was a potentate rather than a prison escapee, I'm seated at a walnut table across from the Governor of the state where I'm wanted by every law dog. And speaking of law dogs, it turns out the man seated nearby, who the Governor has introduced as Stefan Clevenger, is a federal marshal and is acting as the Governor's bodyguard. He studied me with some interest, but has yet to clamp the chains on me. Clevenger is a good-sized man with shoulders wider than normal for his height, and hands, crooked nose, and a cauliflower ear like a prize fighter—scarred knuckles and corncob size fingers. I'd guess he's not a man to toy with.

The train car is something to behold: rich walnut rubbed to a shine, red velvet on some walls and upholstery, and polished brass trim. Even the window glass is beveled and panes at either end of some plain ones have, appropriately, horns-of-plenty filled with fruits and flowers acid-burned into them.

I'm still in my rough clothes, but should have my dude duds on as I'm enjoying my first two fingers of fine brandy and munching on something called almond nuts, which I've never seen before. Mary Ann Merriweather, still sobbing off and on, and Mrs. Hoolihan are partaking of lemonade and some snacks. All this while, Governor and Mrs. Hoolihan extol my virtues. I'd have bet you a dime against my new diamond stick pin that I'd join that smiling man on the moon before this would ever take place. I guess both the good Lord and the heinous Devil work in mysterious ways.

I've noticed, having one ear turned to the ladies, that Miss Mary Ann has said nothing about being violated by that Scroggins lowlife. Unless she bemoaned her fate before I joined up with them, she's keeping it totally to herself. A bit of secrecy I'll honor.

The express train has roared on by, but a regional is close behind, dropped off its caboose and is backing up to hook us up ahead of it, then to haul the Governor's car and the five of us back to Reno from which it came when the gentleman learned of his wife's abduction.

Months ago, I was sucking down gruel in a cold cell. Today I'm sipping fine brandy and eating salted almond nuts in the Governor's private railroad car. Dang if life ain't strange. And I'm worried it'll be stranger yet if I'm soon back in that cold cell with the warden wishing he could add years to my life sentence for escaping. Of course, I could be waiting to hang for defending myself against that crooked sheriff. I guess things could be worse —lots worse.

The Governor's car only has one bedroom, with a bed that looks like the King of Siam should be perched in the middle of it, with half his court joining him. The rest of us are in the lounge portion, with a divan for Miss Mary Ann, and rollout pads on the floor for Clevenger and myself.

I awake more than once to hear Miss Mary Ann sobbing. Dang if I know what to say to her. It pains me to the quick that she seems to be hurt so deeply. I'd like to comfort her in some way, but I'd guess the last thing she needs is a man nearby.

We arrive in Reno in the middle of the night, awakened by the clanging and rattling of the car being switched to a side rail.

It seems the rest of them have elected to sleep the night out where they are. I've decided it's a good time to bid my goodbyes but don't bother to awaken anyone to do so. Rather I slip out and make my way on foot into the center of the little village. I find a hostler, slip into his barn and, still in my rough clothes, flop down in a pile of loose hay to sleep out the night.

I'm awakened in the creeping light of dawn with a shotgun poking me in the chest.

"Can I help you?" I ask, trying to focus on the old boy with the double barrel. When I do, I quickly check to see if he has a star pinned to his vest.

He doesn't.

"The question ain't ..." he growls, "... if'n you can help me. The question is what the Billy Joe hell are you doing in my barn?"

He backs away as I rise and brush the hay off my clothes. Then I answer with a growl equaling his. "Is this a livery or your personal abode?"

"It's a livery, you damn fool."

"Watch your mouth, old man, or a potential customer will find a more friendly place to do business." The old boy was brindle-topped at one time, I surmise by what freckles I can see. Now his pork chop sideburns and handlebar mustache are mostly gray. His neck and chin are shaved clean. Had I a receding chin as does he, I'd whisker it up, but to each man his own.

He guffaws a little. "You talk mighty brave for a fella on the receiving end."

"Do you want to sell a mule and a horse? If not, I'll take my leave and thank you for the accommodations—such as they were."

The barrels are now pointed straight down. "Why the hell didn't you say you was a buyer?"

"Hard to talk with double barrels looking you down."

"I got mules, horses, donkeys, and a by-God Camel. What's your pleasure?"

"I have a horse coming in when that posse returns from hunting those train robbers. Should be among those on the stock car. A palomino with a white blaze on his nose. I'll buy a horse and mule or a good pack horse, if the price is fair, but I'll also expect you to claim that horse coming in for me, and corral and feed him until I return."

"How long?"

"Maybe a day, maybe two weeks. How much?"

"If it's a day, a half dollar. If it's two weeks, a quarter dollar a day."

I extend my hand and we shake. "Now, as I'm hungry for some breakfast, let's see what you've got for sale so I can get on to a cafe."

After dickering with the old boy, who I now know as Clevis and who doesn't mention his last name, I'm the proud new owner of a handsome dun-colored molly mule and a steel-gray gelding. The molly, which is named Molly, seems as sweet as hard candy, but I've been fooled by mules before. She's a molly and as I've said before, one would likely never understand her. That said, my fifty dollars for mule, pack saddle, and canvas paniers seems well spent. And I'm not displeased by forty dollars for the gray, who is called Rocky. Appropriate, as he's the color of granite. I hardly have enough gear to weigh down the saddlebags on Pal, should I regain him, but plan to not suffer the discomfort of ever again riding into the wild without food, water, and a decent bedroll. One never knows when the wild might call as opposed to be captured and returning to a cold cell, or hangman's rope. I'll sleep under a rock in a snake's lair before going back.

Now I need to fulfill my promise, find Shivers Flannigan and deliver his deed, his share of the reward, and his brother's personal items. But that can wait until after breakfast.

Porky's is a clapboard wall-and-canvas roofed facility with the kitchen in a small shed a few steps from the rear door. One would guess Mr. Porky might have been burned out at one time or the other and is now extra cautious with his cooking fire.

That said, and the place being anything but fancy, the cackleberries, side pork, and biscuits are more than merely passable. And the coffee keeps coming. I tip a nickel on top the two bits and head for the station house where the goods I sent ahead should be waiting.

The station master provides me with an envelope and a canvas bag containing, among other things, Slade Flannigan's Derringer and shaving gear. I'm informed that Shivers Flannigan is in Virginia City, running a saloon called The Silver Belle.

I'm a little surprised to see a poster among the two dozen on the station's bulletin board regarding a scruffy-looking Jack Brannigan. Seems someone wants me pretty badly to have spread wanted posters this far. I comment to the station master that it's a rough-looking bunch pictured on his wall, and he agrees.

I'm also informed that the Governor and his party have boarded a stage to Carson City, and I'm a bit surprised to receive a note from the Governor and a letter in a fine hand from Miss Mary Ann. I'm saddened to learn she's on her way to Sacramento City on the Transcontinental where she'll board a river boat to Oakland. She asks me to call on her, am I ever near.

And I was about to decide having a well-educated woman around was to my liking.

Not my first disappointment in life, but the loss of her leaves me feeling hollow and a bit lost.

Now to find Shivers Flannigan.

CHAPTER 26

I VISIT THE MERCANTILE AND LEAVE RENO WITH MOLLY'S paniers half full of good vittles, new ammo, my newly acquired shotgun thanks to a recently departed train robber, a spare Smith and Wesson revolver from another robber, and a bedroll which—when used for the first time—will rival anything I've slept in for a good long while, including the bedroll on the Governor's floor.

Virginia City, Nevada, is an easy ride over undulating desert, fairly barren except for grass and low shrubs, and still with lots of Spring green. The smell of dove weed and the dusty odor of blown sand is much preferred to that of cold creeping mold on hard stone walls and floors. The town is only twenty-five miles on a road heavily traveled with ore wagons and stages. I'm passed by a dozen wagons, that many horsebackers, and two stages by the time I clomp into the bustling, frolicking silver town. The Comstock, I soon learn, is producing millions in silver, and several other mines are doing well. The town itself is four times the size of Reno, having been rocking along since the boom which began in 1858, only a few years after I was born. I'd guess it, on first glance, to be twenty blocks long and ten blocks wide. Seems like every third building is a mill. The city vibrates with rock grinding and eyes water from smoking smelters.

Most the commercial buildings that aren't providing lumber for the mines—ricking and shoring timbers—are mills or smelters, or saloons. I pass at least a dozen saloons and bawdy houses on my way to where I'm informed The Silver Belle is the ground floor of a solid two-story brick building. Pleasure ladies wave at me from windows, dressed in red, purple, and yellow frill and finery with feathers in their hair. Many an ostrich in some foreign land has given up its warmth so these hard-working, health-risking girls can attract customers. Most of them making a living in the only way they know how —the only opportunity that's available to them to get by in this rough and tumble world.

As one might expect from a town with plenty to guard and protect, I pass at least four fellas with copper badges, all sporting sidearms; one with a coach gun at his side.

The Silver Belle is a relatively respectable place with a restaurant on one side with real tablecloths, and two dozen upholstered stools in front of a long bar with a brass footrail. A mirrored glass framed into the backbar is between shelves lined with more than two dozen labeled bottles, and multiples thereof—many of which I've never seen before. Kegs of beer have spigots topped with knobs carved to represent a bull, a bear, an Indian, and a hog. The place has the standard barrel of goober peanut shells barroom-center with a half dozen little tin buckets hanging from its rim. Shells litter the floor, not only near it, but on every square foot of the plank floor. Four gambling tables—faro and a wheel of chance—line the wall opposite the bar, and eight round tables surrounded by benches, with ladderback and captain's chairs, are scattered between. There's a small platform at the rear of the place next to a hallway leading out the back where I imagine occasional entertainment perches.

As it's an hour from sundown, the place is only blessed with a dozen or so patrons, three of them at a faro table, two at a wheel of chance, the rest at the bar.

My eyes grow accustomed to the dim-lit interior, and I can't help but break into a grin so wide I wonder if my face will split. Jasper Todd Jefferson is at the end of the bar, his broad back leaning against the back wall where he can see all that's going on in the place, a sawed-off scattergun leaning on the wall beside him.

By the time I reach him he too is smiling.

"Don't I know you?" I say, and extend a hand.

"Big John Lincoln," he says, as we shake, and he asks, "And you?"

"Brad Jackson, out from the East to buy ranches for some folks back that way."

He laughs and slaps his thigh, then turns to the bartender, a tall skeleton of a fellow with an Adam's apple so big it looks as if one swallowed got stuck about voice box high.

"Bones, be bringin' my old chum here three fingers of the good stuff."

The tall man nods and pours me five fingers. "Friend of yours?" Bones asks.

"Met him a time or two," he says, and laughs again. Then he turns to me, "What brings you to this here Virginia City?"

"Looking for an old friend. And I need to find a fella that's supposed to be running this place—Shivers Flannigan."

"Not here, but will be in about 9:00 p.m. when the place will be packed with miners, drummers, and town folks. I got my supper break coming up. How about I buy you a fat beef steak and we catch up?"

"Fine with me, but I'm buying. First I got to find a place to stable my horse and mule and to bed down for the night."

"We got a corral a block away, with a loafing shed and a third of it's empty. I got a room up in the gables, the attic, and it's big enough for a platoon of soldiers. You ain't paying for some bed-bug hotel."

"Then I know I'm buying that beefsteak."

We find a table at the saloon restaurant far from others, and laugh and tell tales for more than a half hour, downing a couple of chewy but flavorful steaks, beans, stewed tomatoes, hard sourdough bread, and slices of pie made from dried plums. Then I drop my personal gear from the critters and haul it up two flights of stairs to Jasper's—I mean Big John's—garret room. His place takes up a fourth of what was only an attic, he tells me, but has gable windows that look over the street. It's better than fine. It pleases me to find a loose floorboard and I hide my valuables between joists. My gear, still in saddlebags, and my carpetbag, I throw in a corner. I lead Molly and Rocky to their new place, which is a fifty by one-hundred-foot lot divided into three corrals and a small shed that's full of fine hay. My animals have their own individual corral. I fork them a generous two forkfuls and check the trough that is split between two of the corrals.

Good fresh water pleases me and them, and they soon have muzzles buried in it.

Then I head back to the saloon, find a spot at a faro table and play conservative. I'm wishing there was a blackjack table and learn there's one a half block away at Bernice's French Parlor—a fancy name for another saloon not quite so fine as this one.

I wander there and play for an hour, leaving not so fortunate as the last time, but only donating four dollars. But at a dime a hand that's quite a bit of losing. I'm wondering if my nickname is correct, but it matters little as I'm now Brad Jackson. I return to The Silver Belle and the faro table.

When a dapper-looking fellow in a cutaway coat, brocaded waistcoat, striped trousers, and a silk four-in-hand enters, Big John waves him over and whistles at me.

He introduces me to Shivers Flannigan, and I tell him why I'm here. He invites me over to the restaurant as he's yet to eat his supper. I spin the tale of his brother's death and the fact I have a deed, some personal belongings, and his brother's three-hundred-eighty-dollar share of the reward, up in Big John's room. I've had a couple too many, so I have coffee while he eats.

"I got word of Sam's death," he says, shaking his head. "Sounds like he went down fighting."

"Dang rights he did. He saved lots of folks as those stage robbers would likely have killed us all. He was a brave man."

"Brad, you don't know the half of it. He went from private to captain serving in General Grant's army. Then to die at the hand of some thief makes me heart sick. Fact is he had some trouble over in Bismarck and had a poster out on him. That's why you knew him as Slade."

I nod and don't mention Slade and I had something in common. But I do try and console him a little. "The one shot him went down to suffer a good long while and we left him and others for the buzzards."

"Good. I only wish it had been me that shot him. I'd have made sure he died slow."

So, I embellish the tale a little. I actually believe I shot the one who shot his brother, but I let him believe his brother did the deed, and add, "The rotten som'bitch that got a lucky shot on your brother wiggled and moaned for more than an hour, crying like a dog with his nuts in a crack."

"That makes me feel lots better." He stares out the window at the dark street for a long moment, then turns back to me. "That deed you carry is him giving me his majority interest in The Silver Belle. I'm indebted to you for bringing it. He had a diamond stick pin. I don't imagine you've seen it?"

CHAPTER 27

I ALMOST GET RED IN THE FACE, FEEL THE HEAT ON MY NECK, then answer, "Fact is, he gave it to me as payment, with my promise to deliver what I have nearly already done. But if you think ...."

"No, no, it was Sam's wish you have it. Fact is, it belonged to our father ...."

"Then you've got to have it."

"That stone is worth two hundred fifty dollars if a dime. I'll pay ...."

"No, sir. I never had a family to speak of. I value the fact some folks did, and I want you to have your father's ...."

"Look, I'll owe you if you won't let me pay you. You've got a big favor coming."

I laugh. "Don't matter. Dang if I've brought myself to wear it. Too fancy for this ol' boy. It's up with the rest of your brother's things, in ..." I start to say Jasper's room then catch myself, "... in Big John's loft."

"You here in Virginia City for work, or do you need some?"

"I could use some honest work. What do you have in mind?"

He gives me a knowing smile. "Sounds like you're not afraid of a little gun work, should the occasion arise."

"Never have been, should the occasion arise."

"Big John has been sitting shotgun since the day after he arrived in town. He's working too many hours. It looks like easy work, but there's more to it than appears. You've got to keep order in the place, but a cudgel works way better than a scattergun. Hell, you shoot that blunderbuss in the place, and you're liable to kill your target and a half dozen other innocent customers. It doesn't pay to kill off your customers," he laughs, and I join him.

"I'd guess not," I say. "No profit in paying a digger and planting folks who would have paid you."

"So, you'll take the job?"

"I will, for a while. Don't count on me for more than a month or so. Long time plans are not on my agenda, if that will work for you?"

"Works fine, as I owe you."

"Let's go get your stickpin, money, deed, and what not."

He nods, and we do.

So, I've gone from a man in a cold cell to a friend of the Governor and his wife to a man entrusted with a shotgun and keeping the peace.

The hell of it is, I'll be hard put to pull the trigger on some no-good who's raising hell in a saloon, unless he's got a knife at somebody's throat or trying to rob the place. So far, I've gotten away with lots of gun work, but it damn sure calls attention to yourself and, in my situation, that's not a good thing.

The fact is when you're having to stop and count up the men—even if no-goods—you've knocked off their hind legs with lead, the odds are that some fateful time you're gonna miss, and the owlhoot you've been staring down won't.

As I think on it, I'm beginning to wonder about myself? You'd think a fella looking at the business end of Winchester or Colt would waiver, but my wavering always is tardy. Sometimes even the next day when I think back on it, and the fact I could have just as easily made the ground sticky with my innards and juices, I'm wondering. Is a man right in the head when he doesn't quiver at the muzzle of a weapon? I hope I'm not losing all touch with caring if I live or not, and me barely having lived at all with seven of my twenty-six years looking at cold stone walls. Looking back over your shoulder to see who or what's gaining on you, probably with blood on their mind, is bound to make a fella short-tempered and maybe long on mean. Then again, there are times I'm proud of myself, like recently bringing the ladies out of harm's way. And giving up that diamond stick pin, rightfully mine, to a son who seemed to want a keepsake of his father.

When we return, Flannigan heads to his office where he says he's got a safe and I go to an empty seat next to Big John.

"You interested in training someone in your line of work?" I ask.

"What's you mean?" he says.

I laugh. "Seems I'm your new apprentice."

"Dang, that's fine as frog hair."

"So, how does a little fella like me keep the peace without killing the customers."

"You're big as most 'em, but the trick is smile like they be jokin' you," he says, and gives me a big one, then adds, "Smile right up to the time you club 'em up aside the head if need be."

I've got to give that one a laugh, but I can see how that would work. I watch him until well after midnight. He only has to get off his bar stool twice, and both times a smile and a simple request to quiet down or stop the arguing works—or maybe it's the shillelagh, an ax handle, in his big old hand. I do see him lay one of those ham-sized hands on a fella's shoulder and give it a little squeeze one time. The way the miner winced you'd have thought Big John whacked him with the ax handle that rests on the bar above the scattergun. But it was only a little squeeze.

I'm introduced to four barmaids. I notice that two of them exit the back door with customers and are back in the time it takes me to finish my beer. Mary Malone is a buxom girl with a cleavage that would hide a beer mug. Twyla, who doesn't seem to have a last name, is a redhead with a pair of braids to her skinny butt. Freda Hampshire is a flat-faced brunette who looks as if she's part Indian or Mexican. Wanda Hall, so short she could park under my arm, is a giggler, and she seems popular. She's out to the back at least four times that I notice.

I soon note that fellas have to buy a two-dollar token at the bar to trade for a poke, and when the ladies turn it in, they're paid a dollar. Watching little Wanda pocket four tokens in half that many hours, I'm wondering if I might have been born with the wrong equipment to get rich. Of course, there's mean customers and the pox to contend with, so I conclude I'm content with how things are.

I've had a long day in the saddle and am carrying a pound or two of road muck—muck that's likely fifty percent road apples—so hours before he's finished and they've closed up, I roll out my bedroll on the garret floor and am sawing logs. I only stir when I hear Big John clomp up the stairs and enter. And then only for long enough to open and close my eyes.

And he's sawing logs when I arise, seeing light streaming in his window. Today I've got to find a tub to scrub off the countryside and a Chinaman to scrub the same off my duds.

The Silver Belle's restaurant side is not open for breakfast, but the back door is ajar and I leave that way. I see that Sally and the other girls working as barmaids have a destination out back as there are four eight-foot by eight-foot clapboard cribs in the yard behind the place, between it and a pair of privies clearly marked with half-moons painted on the doors.

The back yard is fenced, but there's a gate with a swivel latch. I exit, letting it close behind me.

I wander up 'C' Street until I see a café on a side street with a buggy and several horses at its hitching rail. I wander that way.

The hand-painted sign over the doorway says Gustavo's Cocina, and it seems I'm lucky to find a seat in the little place. There's only one available at a counter with a dozen chairs and none at the six tables. There must be over thirty partaking of Gustavo's chow.

It seems I'm lucky with meal mates as I'm seated

when I swivel to the right and nod to a barrel-chested fella with a brass badge on his twill coat. He has a droopy eye and lips the size of fat oysters but not so firm.

He's busy stuffing his face with some concoction of eggs and meat but glances at me as he's saucering and sipping some hot coffee and nods.

I return the nod and ask, "What's that you're eating, if you don't mind my asking?"

"Chorizo and eggs. The way Gus makes it, it'll burn till it hits bottom, so don't order if you don't want all the bugs in your gut killed dead."

I smile and nod. "Believe I'll try mine sunny side up."

"His mama makes the best tortillas in the west, so don't miss 'em."

"I won't." A chubby senorita is in front of me and smiling, so I order, "Steak, don't murder it, pink and juicy please, and ham if not, and eggs sunny side up or basted a little."

"Coffee, of course?" she says, with an accent, and I nod.

"Ain't seen you about?" the man with the badge asks. I guess it's just the nature of lawmen.

"Just rode in from Reno."

"Don't say. You come on the Transcontinental?"

I extend my hand. "I'm Brad Jackson, and you'd be?"

"Micah Sweeny, deputy city marshal."

CHAPTER 28

"NICE TO MEET YOU." I SAY IT, BUT IT DOESN'T SOUND convincing. I'm getting pretty good at acting nonchalant in the presence of those who might march me back to the hoosegow and to a hangman's rope. But sometimes my worry must show through. And this butt-ugly lawman is a little insistent for my taste.

"You didn't answer. You come on the Transcontinental?"

"Fact is," I say, with a bit of a smirk, "I came from the east on Governor Hoolihan's private car." I don't say only a few hundred miles east.

"The hell you say? Governor of what?"

"Why, of the Territory of Montana," I say, and it comes out haughty, like I meant it to be and like I'd think anyone who rode in on the Governor's car would be.

"How about that," he says, shaking his head. "The Governor give you the boot, or what?"

I look down my nose at him. "Matter of fact, I took my leave to come help a friend out here in your town."

My food comes as he finishes up and unfortunately

has no more need to chew between words. "And who might that be?"

"You know, Mr. Sweeny, if you weren't a lawman I'd think you curious to the point of being a bit on the rude side."

"Part of the job, Mr. Jackson. Part of the job."

"I guess a lawman would know where a fella could find a bath and someone to clean up his clothes?"

"Two blocks, that way," he points. "Mr. Chan, Hot Water, Steaming Clothes, the sign says, whatever the hell that means."

He's being helpful, so I answer his question. "Since you asked, Mr. Flannigan, over at The Silver Belle."

"Doing what? You scrubbing pots and pans?"

"Sitting shotgun."

He nods. "Well, sir, be sparing with that firearm. And that club they use. Last year we had a fella knocked silly by a shotgun guard and the jury found the guard guilty of assault. He's still in our little jail. You ever been in jail, Mr. Jackson?"

I look at him like a bull at a bastard calf, and snarl, "You know, Mr. Sweeney, if you're so interested in me maybe you'll want to wire Carson City and have someone ask Governor Hoolihan about Brad Jackson?"

"Don't take offense." He smiles, but with only half his face and it comes off as a smirk. "If'n I mean to offend you, you'll have no doubt about it."

"I don't doubt it now. I believe I'll finish my breakfast a'fore it goes cold."

"And I'll drop by The Silver Belle later on, after dark, and see how you're getting along. By the way, my lady friend works there. I'll depend on you keep a close eye out on Freda. You'd be well served to make sure no one gives her trouble."

"Help yourself about dropping by. And I'll be watching out for all the ladies and everything else that goes with the job. Nice jawing with you." I turn to my plate. I don't say that Freda obviously has lousy eyesight or she wouldn't be known as this lout's lady friend.

I hear him give a grunt, and he stands and exits.

It's an excellent breakfast with my eggs perfect and a beef steak half as big as the plate covered with what they call salsa—some tomato and pepper concoction—and I'm a little surprised to get tortillas slathered with chocolate. The coffee's so strong it damn near floats the spoon. Forty cents seem a steal so I leave a dime tip and get a smile from the senorita that says "I'd like to know you better," but then dime tips do that. Maybe just positive thinking on my part.

I walk the town up and down the hilly side streets, taking note of Mr. Chan's, messing about until eleven o'clock when I know The Silver Belle opens. Then I report to Bones, the bartender, as I was instructed.

He extends a hand. "Welcome, pardner," he says. We shake and he continues. "I'm on until seven. Shivers gave Big John the day off since you came aboard. He's been working fifteen hours a day and is due. You got a long day ahead of you. When you want to eat send one of the girls to fetch you something from next door and you'll eat at the bar."

"I'm on duty," I say, and walk down to where Big John had been on the end stool. I pick up the shotgun, check the loads and give the two-foot chunk of ax handle a heft.

The place only has a dozen at lunch on the saloon side, but the restaurant side fills up.

Shivers Flannigan, my new boss, wanders in and climbs up on the stool beside me.

"You gettin' situated?"

"So far it's no hill for a stepper."

He smiles. "It's a little like being a lawman, hours and hours of boredom, but when the bull crap hits the fan, it can be pure hell."

I have a thought and have been meaning to ask him, "I don't suppose you're related to any Flannigan's over Phillipsburg, Montana, way?"

He gives me a curious look. "Fact is I am. Mrs. Rosy Flannigan is my sister-in-law. You know Rosy?"

"Best pies and pasties in Montana," I reply.

"I thought you were from back east?"

"Passed through Philipsburg while searching for some ranches for some folks back east."

He again gives me that curious stare. "You're a land agent?"

"Not by profession. Just happened to know some businessmen and they knew I was coming west, so ...."

"I'm going over to eat," he says, seeming satisfied. "You want me to bring you something?"

I give him a shake of the head. "No, sir. I'll do my job until the crowd slims down."

"Good. See you tonight."

There aren't that many folks out west, particularly in the territories, but still that's a hell of a coincidence. I'm sure Jasper—I mean Big John—didn't say anything to Shivers as he never met Rosy. And it's likely a good thing he didn't as I expressed my concern that she might have said something to the law about me being in town, or to the som'bitches, Max or Horace Harrington, and got me thrown in the Phillipsburg pokey. But then again, I may be misjudging her.

After nearly two months of sitting shotgun, getting free beer and lunch and supper, and being surrounded by four pretty barmaids who double as pleasure ladies, I'm getting partial to my job. If it weren't for the damnable heat and the foul air from the smelters, I'd be thinking I'd go to my dotage in Virginia City, Nevada.

I've thought often of the two ladies who have come into my life. Rosy Flannigan, strangely my boss's former sister-in-law, former if a death ends that relationship, and far more often of Mary Ann Merriweather. Other than female companionship—I haven't partaken of the pleasure ladies as the pox seems too prevalent—it's been a satisfying and fairly profitable two months. I'm actually over forty dollars ahead at the blackjack tables down the road. And I'm able to save almost all my two-dollars-a-day wages.

But like all good things, it must come to an end.

CHAPTER 29

IT COST ME TWO DOLLARS TO THE FELLA WHO RODE PAL from Reno the twenty-five miles to Virginia City leading his own horse, but he delivered him in fine shape. He also delivered a bill for the two bits a day I owe Clevis, the hostler who cared for Pal. I gave him the coin and trusted him to deliver it on his return.

I do learn from him that the posse and soldiers returned with five prisoners and a good portion of the loot from the mail car. But am not pleased to discover than their leader, Slippery Savannah Scroggins, I've learned he is called, has not been killed by my hand but has slipped away. I'd like to have him in my gun sights but with luck will never see him again.

I've fought shy of any trouble in town or in my job, doing pretty dang well with talking fellas out of causing trouble or at least talking them into taking it outside.

The city marshal, Tom Bob Thornson, has wandered through a time or ten, and the deputy marshal I sat next to while taking my first breakfast in town has wandered through every night and jawed with Freda for a short while. Only one time did he stop by my barstool, but that time he poked me in the chest with a fat finger and even his droopy eye got wide as he growled, "I don't like the way you treat Freda. You'd best ...."

I grab the finger and twist, and he yowls. "I haven't said ten words to Freda, and I don't poke folks with my finger. I would appreciate it you paid me the same kindness."

"Ya, ya," he says, and he's shaking his gun hand to rid himself of the hurt rather than reaching for the ugly revolver he carries.

As he's exiting the place, I hear Bones behind me. "Jackson, that wasn't the smartest thing you've done since filling that barstool."

"Sir?" I reply.

"That turd, Sweeny, is dumb as one, but he hangs on like a cockroach and is mean as a tarantula. He won't forget you shamed him. Be careful."

"Thanks, Bones, I will," I say, but know it was a dumb move. Times are, I just can't help myself.

IT'S NEAR MIDNIGHT, and Saturday, and we've been packed with miners, drovers, drummers and city business folks since 6:00 p.m. Not only is the air bad from the smelters, but the cigar smoke is hanging down from the sculpted lead ceiling to head high to a seated man. On Saturdays, we have a banjo player and every once in a while, one of the doves squawks out a song. Jenny Lind they are not, but enthusiasm counts.

I sigh deeply as the voices at a table with four card players erupt in condemnation and accusation. I hope the problem it will take care of itself, most do if the shotgun guard is patient. When I finally walk to the table where the heated argument is underway and growing, cudgel in hand, they pay no attention. One tall raw-boned gent in a starched white shirt, gold cuff links, hard collar and silk four-in-hand, with an angular face that looks chiseled from granite, has another smaller puffy-faced fella by the collar. He's shaking his fist in the smaller man's face, which is turning red. I know the small man, Rosco Miller, who's one of the more successful barbers in town and owns his own parlor. The raw-boned lout is tall, not bulky, but not thin either. And he's packing what looks to be a brand-new Colt Peacemaker with ivory grips. It's engraved. It's an expensive piece. Even more so, I'd guess, than the one I lifted from Harrington. So far, he hasn't placed a hand on it. I know Rosco to go firearm-naked so if angle-face draws, it's a one-way affair—not that Rosco may not have a straight razor near at hand.

Per Big John's advice, I walk up smiling. Big John is off this night, not feeling up to snuff, and at the moment, I'm wishing he was backing me up.

With a smile, I say, "Hi, gents. You fellas are getting a little rambunctious ...."

Angle-face is not smiling. "Go the hell back to your corner. This is between this pipsqueak and me."

"Well, sir, I know Mr. Miller here, and I've never known him to be out of line."

"And I am?" the big fella says. He releases Rosco and rises, glaring down at me as he's a half head taller, and now with a hand on his Colt.

I'm still smiling, although it feels like I'm stretching

my face. "Didn't say that, pilgrim. How about you come on over to the bar and let me buy you drink?"

He guffaws a little, then curls a lip as he talks. "And I don't drink with no pissant saloon swamper. Go about your business." He's hunkered shoulders forward, like he's about to pounce.

I take a deep breath and try one more time but am getting weary of the grin. "How about I buy you that drink? You can drink it alone at the bar, if you prefer."

"How about you bring your mama or sister over my way so I can have a little poke ...."

I don't have a sister, but the comment about my sainted ma, even if she had—or maybe because she had —become a lady of the night, turns my badger loose. Before he can lift the Colt an inch, I part his slicked-back hair with the ax handle. He windmills his arms as he stumbles back and crashes over a table surrounded by six hard-drinking miners, all still in dungarees from a Saturday mucking silver ore.

They take umbrage at their drinks being spilled and, before his eyes stop spinning from the blow, they whack on the old boy from all angles. I don't hurry to save him from the onslaught as I'm still fuming from the ma and sister comment. And when I finally move to stop it, he's on his knees, bleeding from eyes, ears, nose, and a split in his lip you could slip a quarter into. Not to speak of an inch-and-a-half gash on the top of his noggin from my cudgel. Blood is running into his eyes from my work and dripping on the floor from that of others.

He's a mess. I stuff the cudgel in my belt and help him to his feet. I get his arm over my shoulders, when one of the miners decides they should be compensated for the drinks and tries to get a hand in angle-face's trouser pocket.

I'm loaded with a beat and bleeding man, who can barely stumble, but do manage to kick the miner where it might discourage him from trying one of the soiled doves. His eyes go saucer-wide and he doubles over holding his crotch with both hands, then goes to his knees.

And the other five come after me like bumblebees after a daisy.

I throw my burden aside, which blocks at least two of them, and grab my ax handle out of where I've stuffed it into my belt. I'm backing up until I'm against the wall and not doing bad. Thank the good Lord, only two of them can confront me due to tables on either side.

A burly Dutch-looking miner, with sandy blond hair sticking beyond his wide face, has just missed breaking my jaw with a roundhouse right from a fist that looks like the sledgehammer I'm sure he uses all day. But the miner to his left lands a straight right to my chest, leaving me gasping for a second. Rather than try to swing at him, I drive it straight. I poke him just under the rib cage burying the ax handle six inches. He "oof's" like a Billy goat has butted him and goes to his knees, blocking a couple of others who want to have at me. In their hunger to get a bite of me, they're falling all over each other.

The Dutchman is coming back, his fists doubled and looking like he's about to devour a bowl of grits—with me the meal—when his forehead explodes and I'm covered with blood and bone. He bounces off my chest and hits the floor like a sack of ore he's carried from the mine. My ears are ringing as I realize someone is shooting.

The one I kicked in the personals is thrown aside by another big black-bearded miner with eyes now like a horse facing a cougar and I think he's after me. But he's trying to make his escape, when I see angle-face is up on one knee with the blood wiped out of his eyes and his smoking Peacemaker in hand. He's doing anything but making peace. The running man takes one between the shoulder blades. Every man and soiled dove in the place are hunting a hideout, or making it through the batwing doors or out the back to the privy—chairs, tables, drinks fly as they're flung aside. Now at least five men are on the ground, and angle-face is calmly feeding a new set of cartridges into his revolver.

"Jackson!" I hear a yell and turn to see Bones has my scattergun. He heaves it my way. By the time I swing on angle-face, he's closing the trap on his Colt and is about to zero in on me. I take two quick strides his way as I've always feared firing the sawed-off in the saloon, as I know its spread is three feet in fifteen. The closer I am, the less additional damage.

I only fire one barrel but know she's loaded with cut up square nails. I realize he and I have pulled off at the same instant. But he's no Bill Hickok, and his shot is not only low but clips my calf on the same leg that has just healed from the gouge across my outer thigh. I glance down and see by the blood it's likely taken a chunk out of my chin bone. I cock the other barrel, limp closer to him and see I can thumb the hammer back down barrel two. He's not only down, but there's a piece of him, the size of my head, missing on the left side below the elbow and above the hip bone.

And the gore is seeping across the floor, shoving and floating goober peanut shells away as it flows.

I'm standing, staring down at the mess that was a man, when my favorite city marshal, droopy-eyed Micah Sweeny, charges up.

CHAPTER 30

"GIVE ME THAT WEAPON," HE YELLS, SO INTO HIS TASK HE'S blowing spittle. He's got an ugly snub-nosed Glasser revolver leveled on my chest, so I shrug and hand the scattergun over without comment.

"Where'd you get the Glasser?" I ask.

"You crazy lout. There's six men on the floor. One of them's a Tupperson, and you want to know where I got my piece?"

"What the hell's a Tupperson?"

"One of four brothers, all gunmen, hard cases."

"Well," I shrug, "there's only three now."

"You're right, and you're damn lucky the others are out of town on a job. They'll be gunning for you. Rupert there was the youngest, and they'll be tacking your hide to the outhouse wall and using it to wipe the dew off'n their lily."

He's right about me taking time to be curious about his unusual sidearm, but I can do nothing but shrug, limp over to my stool and plop down. I turn to Bones, but he's way ahead of me, blows the head off a fresh beer and hands it over. "You likely could use this." Then he hands me a wet towel. "Clean up. You're a mess." I go to work with the rag wiping brains, blood and bone from my linsey-woolsey shirt. Then I ask him for a clean one, pull up my trousers and bind my nicked leg. Luckily, only a quarter-inch deep gouge and no bone damage.

"Get the sawbones, quick," a voice rings out from the back of the place. As if we hadn't already sent for both town docs.

Then, at about the same time, Sweeny and I realize that a fellow is coming from the rear of the place carrying one of the girls. Her head is hanging, black hair flowing down, her red gown growing darker between her breasts, and it doesn't look good.

I leap from my stool and run his way in time to see Sweeny turn white.

"Freda. Oh, no. Freda," he says, then turns to me. "If that scattergun ...." Then turns back and follows the fellow with Freda in his arms out of the saloon.

I don't follow. There's not a damn thing I can do. I'm surprised to see Big John has come down from his loft, and he's at the rear of the place, studying an upended round table. He moves my way, pushing through the crowd that's now standing over the men on the ground. Two of who are moaning and moving; three of who are not.

"Looks like a .44 went through the table where Freda was hiding—not that sawed off."

I exhale a long breath. I damn sure hope he's right. As we're talking, the City Marshal enters with two more deputies who I've done nothing more than trade "howdy" with.

And Shivers is right behind them with one of the town docs on his heels.

City Marshal Tom Bob Thornson walks straight to me. "You know there's a city ordinance against business protection with shotguns."

"Hell, I inherited the job and the scattergun."

"Did you fire it?"

"Yes, sir, I did."

He turns to one of his deputies. "Take Jackson to a cell. I'll be along in a while."

Shivers is close behind him and complains. "Hold on now, Thornson. He was only ...."

"It's your place and I'm sure your damn scattergun—and sawed-off at that. I could be taking you in."

Shivers turns to me. "I'll get to Judge Petersen tonight, and we'll have you out come daylight."

"Doubt it all to hell," Thornson says. Then turns back to his deputy. "Take him."

And we go for a walk. I'm hoping it's not a walk, then a long ride back to Montana.

TRUE TO SHIVERS' word, I'm bailed out in the morning, and Shivers, after telling me that Freda has died in the night, treats me to breakfast at Gustavo's. But it seems she died from a large-caliber bullet, and not from cut-up square nails. This time I try the chorizo and eggs, and Sweeny was true to his word as well. Every bite burns till it hits bottom then burns a while longer.

As we're sipping our coffee at a corner table, Shivers fesses up. "You know I wrote Rosy after we talked about you knowing her."

"And?" I say, a little taken aback.

"She said she might remember you and ask me to send her a better description."

"And?" I ask again.

"And I did, and she said, in her second letter, yes, she remembers you and asked me if I could receive a letter and pass it along to you, unopened."

"And?" I ask again.

"And, that letter hasn't arrived yet. Why was she so insistent I didn't open it?"

I laugh. "Well, I guess as it's none of your business. Truth is, I had eyes for her. Maybe she's sweet on me and doesn't want her ex-brother-in-law to know it."

"My youngest brother's been dead a dozen years. Now I have two dead brothers."

"Well, you know how women are. We'll never understand them."

"Maybe we will, when hell freezes over."

I laugh again, and I, too, am wondering what Rosy has to say and if she suspects who Brad Jackson might be? She knew me as Jack Brannigan, my true name.

We talk for a half hour until the waitress invites us to retire to a bench in front of the place where she assures us, she'll refill our coffee, but Shivers pays up, and we head for the door.

I'm following him out, when I hear someone shout from across the room full of customers.

"Brannigan ... Jack Brannigan," I only turn my head enough to glance that way, and I'm sure it's Fat Freddy Willard. The ugly mean bastard would be hard to mistake. Willard is a guard from Deer Lodge prison; the most hated among many disliked. But I continue behind

Shivers laughing and jawing as if I hadn't just been recognized.

We've gone a block toward The Silver Belle, when I glance back and see Fat Freddy is exiting the place and scanning the routes away. He sees us and follows. He doesn't try to gain on us, merely follows.

What the hell is he up to? I'd guess he only thinks he recognizes me, but isn't sure, and wants to take a better look. I truly have no interest in killing another man, but also have no interest in returning to Deer Lodge, or worse, to learn to do the hangman's dance. I'm pretty sure I'll have to talk like a Dutch uncle to get through the pearly gates as it is.

When we reach The Silver Belle, I glance over to Shivers and tell him I'm going on. "I gotta check on my horses and mule. See you when my shift starts."

"Not today. Big John is back on his feed. You take the day off. You need to catch your breath. Besides, until that hothead deputy calms down, I want you to lay low."

"What hothead?" I ask, as if I didn't know.

"Sweeny, he's been mouthing around that it was you caused Freda's death, and he's gonna even the score."

"Doesn't he know what the doc said, big bullet and all?" It's time for another deep sigh when Shivers just shrugs, so I ask, "How about meeting me out back in an hour. I've got some thinking to do." And I don't mention it, but I have to ditch Fat Freddy Willard before he finds himself a couple of ounces heavier from carrying a pair of .44/.40 slugs.

Damn it.

CHAPTER 31

I PICK UP THE PACE, WEAVE AROUND A COUPLE OF BLOCKS of clapboard houses, and duck down an alley before checking on the stock. Happy to note, Fat Freddy is no longer anywhere in sight. Fat Freddy once clubbed me senseless for the heinous crime of dropping my tin plate and utensils and was known to be the meanest a-hole on our cellblock. A guard who'd club you if a nod would do just as well. To tell the truth, I relish the chance to at least knot his noggin, get his ears to ringing and eyes to spinnin' but know he's trouble on the hoof.

It's time to give my notice at The Silver Belle and move on down the road. Maybe I'll take up prospecting and get rich as Midas. At least get the hell out of Virginia City.

I slip back to The Silver Belle, enter the back way and up the stairs to find Big John snoring away in our room. But he awakens as I enter and pry up the floorboard to recover my valuables. I fill my saddlebags and my now well-worn little carpetbag with my belongings. I still treasure that good suit of clothes, boiled and starched shirt and collar, and silk tie.

Assuring Big John—Jasper—that he's my finest friend, I bid my goodbye with the hopes we'll meet again. Then, with saddlebags over my shoulder, I slip back down the stairs and out to the back to wait on Shivers who promised to show up.

He arrives, on time, and I tell him some of the truth, at least as much as need be, that I had trouble up in Montana and that a fella in the restaurant recognized me and would likely put the law on me. He understands and invites me back to his office so he can settle up my wages.

Unfortunately, when we make our way back in, I have my carpetbag hanging at my side in my gun hand. And there is Fat Freddy Willard at the end of the hall, his sidearm in hand and a ghoulish smile on his fat face.

"Jack Brannigan," he yells. I ignore him and look as if he's yelling at someone else, but Shivers does not. He's slightly ahead of me in the hallway and keeps moving. I stay close behind, presuming Fat Freddy is still not quite sure and won't be firing away when he doesn't know the man between us.

"Excuse me," Shivers says, and tries to step around the big man, purposefully getting in his way, which causes him to weave his weapon away from me for an instant. I use that instant to bring the carpetbag up into the fat man's crotch, then drop it, gaining me a second, as I've whacked him in his eggs and he looks to be considering upchucking. I have no idea if it does much more than distract him, but it gives me that precious second. I drive the palm of my free hand up into his nose, which snaps his head back and sends his hat flying. Now my gun hand is free and, as his head is swimming from the blow to his nose—now spraying blood like water from the corral pump—I drag my Colt and pound the big man up aside his head, just where his fat scalp winkles over an ear.

He staggers back and goes to his back on a table. I'm able to bend and recover his sidearm from the floor.

The big man is tough and is trying to sit back up, so I smack him again with his own stubby revolver. This time, he goes to the floor.

I turn to Shivers, who's standing with his arms folded, seemingly amused. "Give my pay to Big John and tell him to have a fat steak on me. I'll see you on down the road somewhere. And you've got to warn Big John. This man is a big risk to John as well. He should lay low until Fat Freddy is on his way out of Virginia City."

"I will. He can hide out in the loft for a month if need be. Remember," he lowers his voice so Fat Freddy and others at the other end of the saloon can't hear, "I got that letter coming. Drop over to my cabin in a few days, and I'll fill you in. But don't show your face in town. Not only this fat man, but the Tuppersons are due back, and they'll be toting a hell of a grudge."

"If I'm in the territory, I will stop by," I say, and don't add that I'm very interested in what Rosy has to say. I shake his hand and take my leave out the back door. I hotfoot it to the corrals, saddle Pal, the gelding I bought from Clevis, hurry the pack saddle onto Molly and load the paniers with my goods from the loafing shed. Then I string out my mule and spare mount and head out past the smelters, crushers, the mine ponds, and small mountains of tailings. To be truthful, as much as I enjoyed the town, I'm happy to be away from the bad air, the elbows of too many folks, and the noise and worry of The Silver Belle. Deer Lodge Prison give me enough of being crowded by other folks.

As I ride into the desert, I know it's truly summer as I'm teased by the sight of lakes in the distance. I know they're the dancing lakes of heat, and many a man has died of thirst chasing them. No matter how you pursue, they're always the same distance away.

I have enough grub for a week, my Winchester, shotgun, and two sidearms, as well as my bedroll and some camp gear including some fishing line and hooks. Two pounds of coffee, flour, and more than a pound of salt. A small cast iron fry pan and tin pot that'll do for brewing coffee. I can live like a potentate, at least for a few days. I'm in fine fettle.

In a day's ride, I know there are some high mountains, pines and firs—cooler weather, clean air—and I could use a little vacation. I believe I'll go fishing and see if I can knock down a fat deer, then put my feet up on a rock by a crystal-clear lake and fill my belly with fried and fire-roasted vittles. Cooler weather will be welcome as its over one hundred degrees most days, now that its July. And hot weather and crowds don't mix. Half the men have the vinegar, old meat smell, and it's revolting. I yearn for high mountain air.

I watch my back trail equal to watching that ahead until Virginia City is out of sight, then give it a glance until even the smelter smoke stacks are unseen, then until even the tendrils of smoke are no longer visible.

No more than five miles from town I see a pile of bones, thinking, at first, it's a deer, but as I near, I see it's human. A skull smiles up at me, seeming to laugh at my enthusiasm for riding into the desert. He's saying "You damn fool, come join me in hell." I give my head a shake as I pass wondering how many times that could have been me, moldering in the desert sun. When you're alone in the wilderness, no one would know you've become worm food. I'm dour for a moment, then laugh aloud, wondering if this fellow's fate was a result of eating Gustavo's chorizo?

Even the smell of him is gone, replaced by the pleasant odor of sage, a touch of moisture in the air, and the hope of rain with clouds on the distant horizon. Dust to dust, ashes to ashes. If no one cares, you could rot, unburied, unmarked, in the desert. The winners would be the buzzards and little critters. You'd likely not care much.

Already I'm feeling better. After a few hours, I'm in the pines and feeling pretty damn good about it.

I come upon a trickle of a stream that disappears into the desert behind me, soaked into the sand. I follow it higher and higher where it widens to five feet before narrowing after more than a mile to only two feet, and I find its source. A fine lake in a little box canyon, surrounded by pines, firs and river willows, all backed by a granite cliff. And dang if there's not a deep wind cave off to the side that will give me shelter, should it storm. Others have camped there as evident by a fire ring of rocks and black smoke stains on the cave walls and roof.

The sky is streaked with pink, yellow and blue, ducks are enjoying the pond and darting about and chattering with raucous quacks with a drake trying to procreate with more than one mate. Frogs begin to show off their vocals with reverberating bleats that would make you believe they were the size of hogshead barrels rather than smaller than your fist, and mourning doves coo in contentment before leaving the shore after their evening drink.

This is how a fella should live out his days.

Had I the company of Miss Mary Ann Merriweather, I'd be in hog heaven. I think on her and sincerely hope she's safe in Oakland and enjoying her employment as a Classics professor. I know she's the envy of all who are fortunate to come in contact with her.

She's part of my life—being touched by her even as only a friend—that I'll likely never forget.

I'm comfortable in my new abode for a full week, staying out of what little weather we've had as it's getting on toward Summer, and rain will soon be only a memory. Having discovered the drawings some former occupants who decorated the walls of a nearby cave with line images of bison, antelope, and deer, having caught more fine trout than a fella could eat in a week, and having rested and relaxed more than I have since I before I was wrongly accused and thrown in Deer Lodge for life, I'm truly relaxed.

I still have had snakes gnawing at my belly on occasion over the past weeks as I've not settled things with Colonel Maximillian Harrington and his son Horace, and maybe I never will. But I won't harbor the hate I felt for them. I've come to the conclusion that doing so may harm me even more than them, and that folks make a good deal of their own Hell right here on earth. I hope that's the Harrington's fate.

That said, should they haphazardly appear before me, I'll likely invite them to draw a weapon.

If it's true you reap what you sow, then they are dealing with their own monsters. I've been happy here for a few days.

I was once told that when you get too comfortable just wait for the other boot to drop.

I've just this morning concluded that I should return to Virginia City and see if my letter has arrived by slipping up on Shivers' cabin in the dark of night. I'm saddling Pal and my other two critters when I look up and see an Indian, hair to his waist, sitting a skunk-striped dun horse, not a hundred feet from me. His rifle rests across his thighs as if I'm no risk. Still ....

My weapons are with my gear back in the cave thirty feet from me. I spin to run for them and am face to face with Virginia City Marshal Tom Bob Thornson, Deputy Marshal Micah Sweeny, and two other boys from Virginia City. I know now why the Indian seemed to have no fear of me.

"That Indian tracker of mine make you a little nervous, Brannigan?" Thornson asks. The fact he's called me by my real name doesn't escape me.

"My compliments on your silent stalking. Y'all could sneak up on a prairie dog standing on his hinds atop his tailings. You're a little out of your jurisdiction, aren't you?" I ask.

"Well, sir, it's amazing how far some fellows might ride to collect a five-hundred-dollar reward."

"Up to five hundred is it? Can't imagine that's still good at all."

"Territory of Montana assures us it is." He turns to

Micah. "Tie this no-good murdering piece of garbage on his horse. We left the town with little law and need to get back at it."

I'll tell you, having your thighs bound tightly to the latigo, your wrists tied behind you, no hat in the heat, and a fellow who thinks you're responsible for the loss of his love, leading you is not my choice of travel. Sweeny is enjoying his retribution a little too much for my taste. Then again, my taste doesn't seem to count for much. He's sailed my hat off into the sage just to watch me burn while we travel. We spend a night with me given one mouthful of jerky and one swig of water, and bound to a tree trunk so tight I imagine my eyes are bulging. Then we ride into Virginia City where I feel like the main attraction in a circus parade as I'm led to the city lockup. Folks are pointing and commenting like I'm a monkey in a cage. I've been there before, in the city lockup, but this time I don't expect to be bailed.

I do get one piece of good news from the sobering drunk in the cell next to me. The three surviving Tupperson brothers—bearing a blood-grudge against me —were the next gang to try and hold up the mail car on the Transcontinental. They were surprised when two dozen soldiers popped up from what looked to be tarpaulin-covered, wheat cars front and back of the mail car, and when a Gatling gun on a flatbed next in line suddenly appeared from under a tarp. The *Virginia City Territorial Enterprise* speculated that twenty pounds of lead was flung at those robbers in less than sixty seconds. All seven of the robbers, and their horses, met their maker in short order and their bodies, what was left of them, were displayed on boards leaning up against the undertaker's establishment in Reno. I'll be surprised if the train is tried again, as word travels fast.

I'm a guest of Virginia City for a full week, having two visits from Shivers and two from Big John, at great risk to himself, when I'm surprised by one from the big man who was a bodyguard of Governor Hoolihan's, Stefan Clevenger.

But I'm not confused for long as he clamps my wrists and ankles in irons. He has the loan of a prison wagon and driver to return me to Reno, where we catch the Transcontinental and retrace my journey back to Virginia City, Montana, then, to my surprise not to Deer Lodge, but rather all the way to Helena.

Mr. Clevenger is not a talkative man, and probably doesn't say a dozen words the whole trip, and he's a cautious one as I'm well chained the whole trip including my trips to the privy, which, on the Transcontinental, is a seat over a hole in the train-car floor.

I'm equally surprised when I'm placed in a cell in Helena rather than promptly returned to Deer Lodge. Clevenger holds all he knows close to the vest. When I'm in place, he hands me a letter, from Rosy Flannigan, he's carried all the way from being handed it by Shivers; and another, to my great surprise, from Miss Mary Ann Merriweather.

And I'm ever more surprised by the contents of both.

CHAPTER 32

A LOT HAS HAPPENED SINCE I RODE OUT OF PHILLIPSBURG.

Rosy's letter informs me that she was Colonel Maximillian Harrington's paramour and is willing to testify to all she knows about Horace having killed the soiled dove that I was accused and found guilty of doing, and of he and his father setting me up for the fall. Willing, she is, as now Colonel Harrington is dead, killed less than a month ago by his own son. And Horace? Horace was hung by the neck only a week ago for the dirty deed. It seems Horace didn't do well in Washington, D.C. and upon his return to Phillipsburg didn't take to his father's condemnation. It seems the Good Book is correct regarding that reaping thing. And I was right as well, as the Harringtons made their own Hell right here on earth —son slaying father then his neck being snapped as his reward. Good enough for the lying sons'a'bitches.

Rosy also informs me that Cornelius Caphorn, the owner of Hard Rock Harry's in Granite, who's now a resident of Phillipsburg, will join her in testifying. Both have written the Judge, Mortimer Allenthorp, who convicted

me, with a statement as to their knowledge of my inno-
cence. With the hope he'll inform the court currently to
try me, of the lies told that began the series of events that
led me to this Helena jail.

I'm to be tried for the murder of Morgan Tuttle, who
was the City Marshal of Phillipsburg, but since he gave
false testimony at my former trial it seems there are some
so-called extenuating circumstances. Even though he was
a lawman it could be construed I was acting in self-
defense. It will be up to a jury to decide.

It takes me a good while to digest all that before I
open the missive from Miss Mary Ann.

I have a proposal.

She begins with, "It seems you saved my life. You
know it's said when you save a person's life you're
forever responsible for them. I won't hold you to that,
but I hope it's true and that you'll spend your life
with me."

It brings tears to my eyes as she still has no idea who I
truly am, what I've done, and where I might spend the
rest of my life as short a time as it might be.

I wonder if her proposal will stand once she learns
the Brad Jackson is really Blackjack Brannigan and is now
a guest of the Territory of Montana in a Helena jail.

But that said, there are extenuating circumstances in
her situation as well.

It seems she's with child.

And being an unmarried lass she will soon be ostra-
cized by all those highly educated folks at Mills College
for Women in Oakland, and will have to leave. It's no
matter her circumstance is not her doing.

She has high hopes that my obvious former endearment will carry over, even though it's obvious she doesn't carry my child.

But as I think on it, the child doesn't know that, nor does anyone else.

The day is full of surprises, not to be exceeded by the last one that comes to me just before I'm normally served my beans, bacon and bread.

A waiter in white coat appears at my cell door carrying a tray, and is followed by a guard who opens my cell and waves me out, with, "You're on your way to the jail office to have supper with some guests."

"Who?" I ask.

"You'll see." The guard says, and his tone is much nicer than it's ever been before.

I'm surprised to see a folding table in the office covered with a white cloth, surrounded by three chairs, and even more so to be greeted by the City Marshal of Helena. Who seems unhappy about not having supper with Governor Norval Hoolihan and his wife Abigale. I am.

Mrs. Hoolihan actually hugs me as if she's my grand-mother, and the governor shakes my hand. I pull the chair out for the missus and take a seat across from the territorial governor.

As we eat a leg of lamb with all the trimmings, they make small talk, then as we sip a glass of brandy, he assures me, "I've carefully reviewed your case, Jack. You're going to trial ...."

"No, pardon, sir?" I ask, my hopes dashed.

"No, it's not politically expedient but I don't think there's a chance in Hell ... pardon me, Abigale ... that you'll be found guilty. That sheriff you shot ...."

"Sir, he shot me at the same time. And was a lowlife who lied at my trial."

"Nevertheless, we know he knew you'd been falsely accused and prosecuted, and gave false testimony. It would take a hard lot of jurists to find you guilty."

We talk on for a while and even though I'm disappointed that I won't be pardoned and immediately released, I have reason to believe I'll be set free in good time.

As he's stands to leave, his wife prods him, "See what you can do for Jack to make him more comfortable."

"Jack?" he asks, following her lead.

So, I decide to be bold. "Governor, I had some valuables. Gold coin and cash. I need to wire some money to the young lady who was with Mrs. Hoolihan. She's now in Oakland."

"How much?" Mrs. Hoolihan asks before he can reply.

"Five hundred dollars," I say.

The Governor clears his throat, glancing at his wife before he centers eyes on me. "The court would normally impound what might be consider ill-gotten gains ...."

"Bull!" Mrs. Hoolihan snaps, then turns to me, "If the Governor," and she almost spits the title out, "won't get your money released I'll personally send it. You can pay me back when you're released."

"Abigale," he sputters, "that won't look good politically!"

She gives him a hard, tight smile, then says, "Then, Norval, it won't look good, but it will happen. If you don't want it to 'not look good' then get Jack's money released."

He again clears his throat. "Even that won't look good,

but .... I guess we could get that much released. After all Jack was working the whole time and has horses and weapons the state could sell."

"Just do it, please, Norval," she says.

I don't smile, but want to. Then I tell her, "Mary Ann is at Mills College for Women in Oakland."

"I know that. I'll take care of it," Abigale says.

"I'm indebted," I say, then I shake hands again. "Thanks for supper. I guess you know where I'll be," I say with a smile, and shrug.

"Not for too terribly long," the Governor says.

As they wave the guard back in, I ask, "One more thing. Can I impose on you folks for some writing materials? I owe a couple of letters."

"I'll have pen, ink, and paper delivered in the morning," he says, and I can see the guard shaking his head in wonder.

As the guard locks me in my cell, he asks, "You related to Hoolihan, or what?"

"No, sir. We spent a little time wandering around Nevada together."

He shrugs, locks me in, and leaves.

It's kind of nice to keep them wondering.

CHAPTER 33

I've written a couple of sentences at one time or another, but I've never filled three pages, until now. And that's just one of the two letters.

I tell my life's story to Mary Ann confessing all and informing her that should she still want to give her child a father, and should I extricate myself from my current situation, I'm her man. I assure her that no one knows of her mistreatment by that Scroggins owlhoot, who I now truly hope was killed by my blow—but know he wasn't as those arrested testified to his flight. As far as anyone will ever know, Mary Ann and I were married in Reno before she went on to Oakland—a status she could tell no one as the College was assured that she was single and would have nothing to keep her from her duties there. A small lie is better for her reputation than an illegitimate birth, no matter the cause.

I also advise her that she can either stay in Oakland or San Francisco—should I be released, I'll join her—or she can come to Helena and join me upon my release.

I fully expect her to take the five hundred dollars and

go back East where I'm sure she has friends where she went to college, far from the stain of an illegitimate child, and to never hear from her again. Who knows?

The next morning, after I'm served a bowl of mush lathered with molasses and a generous mug of coffee, I get another surprise. Life, these days, seems peppered with eye-poppers. This one comes in the form of a well-dressed lout sucking on a meerschaum pipe carved like a walrus head, in white spats, and a bowler hat of the latest style. He introduces himself, with as cold a handshake as the fish that walrus eats, as Percy Appleseed, the author of serials in Leslie's Weekly, dime novels, and penny dreadfuls. He visits me in my cell and brings me the gift of three dime novels he's written. *Wooly Wanda the Woman Mule Skinner; Mad Harry Hanson the Hangman of Harper's Gulch;* and *Wild Willy Wilkerson, Whip Man of the Wilderness.* I laugh at the titles and he insures me that alliteration sells novels. I don't show my ignorance by asking what the hell alliteration might be. The drawings on the covers are exciting.

It seems he wants to write the adventures of Blackjack Brannigan. To be titled *Blackjack, The Blackheart of Blackfoot Country.* I correct him that it's actually Blackfeet, and he corrects me back that it really doesn't matter as Blackfoot reads better. It will be introduced to the unsuspecting public both as a dime novel and a serial. He smiles like the jackal I'm beginning to think he is, as he thinks I'll be proud of that title. Then he suggests ten dollars and I suggest one hundred for my cooperation. He says, after we agree on seventy dollars, I'll be paid ten dollars now and the balance upon publication of the book or the first serial. And he asks if it's true that I've killed twenty men, most in fair fast-draw street or saloon battles. I laugh since I've never seen a 'fast-draw' fair fight and have only read about such a thing in dime novels.

That takes me back a mite, as I can't imagine what an effect a story like that with me having killed twenty men —even if true, which it's not—would have on a jury. So, I decline his generous offer not knowing if it's in fact generous or not, until after the trial. I inform him that my life is not nearly so adventurous as street talk would have it.

"You don't want ten dollars, Mr. Brannigan?" he asks.

"Sure, doesn't everyone. But I don't want it until after the trial."

He clears his throat, then suggests, "And if they hang you. Ten dollars will do you little good then."

I chuckle. "And that sixty dollars you'll owe me when the story gets better with me dancing in thin air?"

He smiles. "Well, sir, I guess we could arrange to have it applied to a fancy headstone."

"More likely, you'll pour a quart of Who Hit John on my grave, after you've processed it through your gut."

"I'm a man of my word, Mr. Brannigan."

"And I'm Queen Victoria's next husband. No, sir, I believe we'll discuss this over a cool beer when I'm a free man."

"As you wish, but can we begin the interviewing?"

"I appreciate your interest. However, I believe I'll wait. Should they find me guilty I can talk fast should I have the usual three days to prepare to meet my maker."

"If you can tell it in that short time it can't be much of a story?"

Again, I chuckle and am tempted to slap my thighs,

but don't. "Fact is, Percy, sure as Hell is hot, it's seventy dollars' worth." I'm pretty sure I can exaggerate as much as Percy can, after all I've been living a lie since I escaped prison.

"Humph," he mutters looking out of my cell for the guard, then turns back to me. "I should tell you, I have an appointment to interview the Governor's wife, who I understand you rescued from villains and killed several men in the process."

I must chuckle again. "As far as I know, no one was killed in that affair. However, I did put some knots on some old boys' heads. The real adventure in that affair came later, when the Governor's men and the military flushed all those rats outta their den."

"But that's not your story."

"But that's the true story."

"Mr. Brannigan, we must, if possible, make this a real adventure. Even if it means embellishing the truth a little."

"You come see me after the trial, Percy, then you can polish it all you want. Of course, we might have to renegotiate the price."

"Blackjack ... may I call you Blackjack?"

"Jack will do, between us friends, Percy."

"Jack, just remember I came to you first."

"And you'll have ... what is it they call it ... the first right ... no, the right of first refusal."

He looks at me skeptically, then mutters, "I'll be in the courtroom."

"See you then," I say, then add, "Give Mrs. Hoolihan, and the Governor if you see him, my regards."

When he leaves, the drunk in the cell next to mine,

pushes his face up against the bars. "You're Blackjack Brannigan?"

"Guilty," I say.

"Hot damn, is it true you've killed twenty-six men?"

I laugh. "Ask me in a week. It's likely to be forty-six and a tribe of Blackfeet savages by then. Killed them all with a buttonhook, I did."

I plop back down on my bunk and open one of the dine novels Percy brought me. If I get nothing else out of my life story other than three short reads and a rope, at least I'll have something to entertain me until my eyes and tongue bulge out.

No more visits from the Hoolihans. No more leg of lamb, for a week. I am visited by Gerald Jesperson, Esquire, who agrees to represent me for the princely sum of one hundred dollars, plus more to be negotiated, should an appeal be necessary.

Mr. Jesperson has a gut the size of a Hampshire Hog, legs like a hippopotamus, fat hands with corncob fingers, bulbous lips, and a nose as wide as a deck of cards that's veined and beet red. If a quart of whiskey is not a daily for him, I'd be very surprised. But he talks as smooth as a sow's ear with a voice that would hypnotize a man out of a dither fit.

"Mr. Brannigan," he says, purring like the alley cat I imagine he is, "I've prevailed in eighty-seven percent of my criminal cases."

"If that's true, Mr. Jesperson, it seems you should refund the advance should I need to appeal, not require more funds?" I'm only half serious, but being in a cell with no one to talk to since the drunk was bailed gives one a twisted sense of humor.

His face is plastered with a smile like a kid who's caught with his hand in the cookie jar, and he laughs a little too loud and sardonically. "That's not the way it works, Mr. Brannigan. I'm told you have far more on deposit with the court than the hundred I'm requesting. So, it should be no problem."

"I do, sir. And now that I know you know that; does it assure me you will not purposefully lose the case then require more money subsequent to me being sentenced to hang. Who wouldn't want an appeal? At that time, I'd guess a prisoner would be ready to sign his all ... hide, hair, bones and all ... over to you to save his hide."

He knifes me with a hard look, as hard as pig eyes can muster. "You've got to trust me, Mr. Brannigan. You'll walk out of the courtroom at my side, not with a deputy flanking you after they've chained you up."

"Since you come with the Governor's recommendation, I'll trust you at least as much as I'd trust any lawyer or politician. I'll tell you what. I'll ask for fifty dollars to be released to you, then you'll get another fifty if we win?"

He guffaws again. "And I'll tell you what, Mr. Brannigan. I believe I'll find someone easier to represent. I only agreed to one hundred as the Governor asked me to treat you kindly. Nice chatting with you. Good luck." He walks to my cell door, but before he can yell for the guard, I cave in.

"Since the Governor sent you, I'll go for the hundred."

He turns, and shakes my hand. Unlike Percy the reporter, Mr. Jesperson has a handshake like he grew up pounding spikes on the railroad. Fat men will fool you that way as they carry most of or all of three hundred pounds around every waking moment.

He spends the next two days grilling me on what happened, and teaching me what to do and not do when I'm seated with a jury on my right, a jury that can turn thumbs up or down like I was in one of those Roman arenas I've read about.

CHAPTER 34

I'm informed my trial is set for three days hence.

And I'm surprised again when I have another visitor. It's only been three weeks since I found myself in this dank dungeon.

She's no less beautiful than I remember. In fact, takes my breath away. Miss Mary Ann Merriweather is ushered into my cell while a guard waits just outside. I presume they don't allow visitors of the opposite sex to provide favors to prisoners.

But I don't much give a hoot and steal my first kiss from Mary Ann before she has a chance to object ... and she doesn't.

"I had to come," she says, looking up into my eyes, causing a heat to sear my backbone and my loins to quiver.

"I hate you did come and love it. I wish I was where I could buy you supper with crystal, that bubbly French wine, and fancy china."

She smiles. "Soon."

"Are you going to the trial," I ask, both hopeful and apprehensively.

"I am. I'm a guest of the Hoolihans in the Governor's mansion, and Abigale has offered to join me. The Governor is scheduled to testify on your behalf. If it looks as if things are not going your way."

"So, I'm to worry if the Governor is called?"

She looks as if she shouldn't have told me, so I laugh. "Heck, I'd be worrying anyway." Then get serious and ask, "How are you feeling?"

"A little morning sickness, but that's to be expected."

"I wish I was there to hold your hand."

"You will be."

They allow us to talk for over an hour. Most visits, other than with your attorney, are limited to fifteen minutes, so I imagine the Governor or Abigale's hands are at work.

Before she leaves, I make a request, "Mary Ann, this stinking jail is no place for a lady, particularly for a lady ... in your condition. I'm fine here and will see you in the court room."

"Are you sure?" she asks.

"I'd prefer it. See you there."

"I'll try and send you some things."

"You can do something that might help. My good clothes are in my carpe bag, with the City Marshal, I understand. Could you have them brushed and hung out so I'm presentable."

"Done," she says, and gives me a hug and another kiss from lips as soft as air and as sweet as honey.

I swear, if they find me guilty, I'll claw my way through these stone walls, as I will be with Miss Mary

Ann or die trying. But I'd prefer to be with her without our having to look over our shoulders.

My suit is pressed, my brogans shined, my shirt ironed and starched, my arm garters holding my shirt sleeves at the proper length, and my silk four-in-hand is spotted and slick and shiny brown as a fresh-born Hereford calf. The Governor even sent his own personal barber to trim my mane and shave me slick.

I could tell that visit by the barber caused some uproar among the guards. It seems they take umbrage at a prisoner getting such special treatment.

A little consternation rolls over me while I'm waiting to be escorted to the courtroom, as I overhear one guard say to another, "This prima donna Brannigan thinks ol' Norval being on his side will get him flying outta here like a sage hen on the wing. I guess he don't know that more than half the town hates the pompous som'bitch. They'll never find a jury who'll cater to anything hard-ass Hoolihan wants. That alone will likely get Brannigan stretched. You know that badge he kilt over in Phillipsburg has kin here in Helena. Well-liked folks so I understand. Rougher than a cob, but well-liked by many."

Whoever he was speaking with spoke up as well. "I'm taking bets we'll be checking the trap door on the scaffold as soon as the trial ends."

They both laugh, but I don't. I hope this doesn't portend a heinous result from the coming festivities.

Those overheard remarks make my mouth go dry for a while, then I reconcile that there's never been a politician, particularly an appointed one like a territorial

Governor, who was loved by all. I can only hope he's loved by more than half my jurors.

I'm escorted in to a wood-paneled courtroom with room for two hundred in the galley and join my lawyer at a table. I am more than a little shocked to see the courtroom packed with observers. It's standing room only; the rear crowded with standers. As the guards have not removed my wrist chains, the instant the entourage is seated after standing for the entrance of the judge, attorney Jesperson approaches the bench along with the prosecutor and I'm pleased by the result, as my wrist chains are removed. Manford Gundersen is the judge, a man I know nothing about. But one Hoolihan referred to as Manny, so I have high hopes he and the judge are chums. Gundersen is gray with a generous head of hair, reminding me of illustrations of our former President Andrew Jackson, and full but well-trimmed beard. Bespeckled, long nosed, steel gray-eyed, and erect, he's distinguished looking.

As soon as Jesperson retakes his seat, I thank him as I rub the pain out of my wrists.

"More than one reason," he whispers.

"What?" I reply.

"Six of Tuttle's relations are in the courtroom. I'd hate to see you having to run for it with chains restricting your flight. No weapons allowed says the sign outside, but those fellas haven't been searched."

Then he goes into his lawyer mode. "Remember what I said about not smiling or looking too confident. The jury is eyeballing you and will take notice of your response. Humility is the keyword."

"Yes, sir," I say, as I glance at the twelve men in the

jury box and give them a nod but no smile. Then I turn and eye the crowd behind and give Miss Mary Ann a wink. I don't see Rosy anywhere, then realize that witnesses are not allowed in the courtroom except to testify. Nor do I see a half dozen fellas who look like they might want to rip my head off and piss down my neck hole. But I can't see to the rear of the packed courtroom without rising.

Witnesses for the prosecution are called, one after another, and if Jesperson says it once, he says it a dozen times, "I object, hearsay." And most times the judge agrees. I've already seen the example of what street talk does, and most of what I hear from the prosecutions so-called witnesses is just that—hyperbole and auxesis, Jesperson calls it. Words I've never heard before, but I'm glad he's smart enough to use them.

Finally, it's the defense who calls witnesses. And Jesperson has only three. First is Cornelius 'Corny' Caphorn who owned Hard Rock Harry's in Granite, and who testified against me at the trial that sent me to prison.

"I lied," he says, and I'm a little surprised he's so frank and forthright. It means he committed perjury. Of course, he is questioned at length by Jesperson and has the opportunity to explain the fact he was under duress, and his wife and children were at risk. He's cross examined by the prosecutor who makes him admit to having been a liar, and suggests he's lying now. But even after the prosecutor's attacks, I'm convinced the jury is on his side, and hopefully mine. He finishes and the judge excuses him.

But not before warning him, "I will take up your

perjury at a later date, Mr. Caphorn. Don't leave Helena until we meet with the territorial prosecutor."

He nods, and is excused. He's taken great risk for me, and I won't forget it.

Rosy Flannigan is called to the stand.

My breath is taken by her testimony. Rosy was well thought of in Phillipsburg, loved by many for her baking skills. I had no idea I was not her only lover, which proves I was the picture of young and naïve.

CHAPTER 35

"I HAD A RELATIONSHIP ..." SHE SAYS, "... WITH MAX Harrington, whose son actually killed the young lady Mr. Brannigan was found guilty of murdering. I overheard Max and his son discussing the killing."

"Objection, hearsay," the prosecutor says, leaping to his feet.

"Let's first hear the circumstance," Jesperson says before the judge can rule.

"I agree," the judge says, and it seems he and the jury, in fact the whole courtroom is hanging on what Jesperson has warned me will be Rosy's salacious testimony. Another fancy word, salacious, which I must look up in the dictionary Abigale Hoolihan kindly provided.

Rosy continues, "Colonel Harrington and I were ... were indisposed ...."

"In bed you told me," Jesperson says, and even I blush. Rosy is the color of her name, keeps her eyes glued to the floor, but she continues.

"Yes, late at night, and his son rapped on the door. He

rose in his nightshirt, stepped outside and closed the door, but I was curious. I went there and could hear clearly as Horace ....."

The prosecutor objects again, but the old judge seems more than a little interested, and snaps at him, "I'll allow this."

And she continues. "Horace is ... was ... the Colonel's son."

"And was hung by the neck until dead for killing his father, correct?" Jesperson says, more a statement than a question.

"Correct. Anyway, Horace was telling ... drunkenly ... Max ... his father ... about accidentally stabbing this soiled dove, and they talked for a long while. His father even made the statement, 'accident, hell.'" She turns to the jury. "Pardon my language, but that's what he said and I'm sworn to be truthful."

She talks for a good long time, about the trial and the fact she wasn't called to testify and, to her great shame, didn't offer to do so. She goes on to tell of her visits to prison and bringing me baked goods. I thought she did so out of love and now know it was guilt.

I can't begin to appreciate what it must have taken for Rosy Flannigan to come forth with this testimony. Likely, in fact no doubt, her business and reputation is ruined. Women, housewives, are half her business and will shun her, and the other half, miners, will consider her a soiled dove and want to take advantage. If I get out of this mess I'll do my best to see she gets somewhere she can start over. She'll have to relocate.

The prosecutor is unrelenting in his attack on Rosy, to

the point it's all I can do not to leap up and go for his throat. Jesperson senses my anger and keeps a hand on my leg, and whispers several times, "relax."

I don't, but hope I appear to the jury to not be a madman, and they don't know the heat flooding my backbone unless it shows in my cheeks.

Mrs. Abigale Hoolihan is the last witness and even though the prosecutor objects time and time again about her testimony being irrelevant, the judge allows it as Jesperson says it "goes to character." I don't mention to anyone, and hardly to myself, that had it not been for her being accompanied by Miss Mary Ann, this character would likely have been heading for Reno rather than to rescue her. Fate has worked in my favor on this occasion, but then maybe I was due.

The jury informs the judge that he should hold folks nearby as they won't be long, and when they're excused Jesperson gives me a furrowed brow and whispers, "That could be bad news. It seems they've already made up their minds." The judge excuses us and says to return after lunch and I'm escorted, in chains again, to my cell across the street from the courtroom and for the first time am confronted by a bevy of Tuttle's kin.

They shout some expletives at me, mostly about how they will enjoy seeing my neck stretched. They're a rough-looking bunch, miners and drovers I'd guess. Maybe bums and moochers. A couple of their women are with them, and they scream things that make my face redden. Their men only laugh as they do.

That, and Jesperson's warning, does not encourage my enjoyment of my beans and beef heart I'm served for lunch. I've barely sopped my plate with the chunk of hard bread accompanying it, when the guards return and chain me up for a return to the courtroom.

The jury is seated and Jesperson nudges me. "They're smiling and looking at you. Good sign."

I take a deep breath and hope he's a good judge of character, and is proven to be when the jury foreman announces, "Not guilty."

The courtroom roars with both cheers and condemnations, and Mary Ann is at my side throwing arms around me at the same time I'm pumping Jesperson's fat hand.

As we exit the courtroom, this time through the front doors, I'm greeted by Governor Hoolihan and Abigale, who also embraces me.

The Governor invites Mary Ann and me to join he and Abigale at Toy's Oriental Emporium over in Last Chance Gulch for a glass of beer and to talk about my future, a subject I haven't spent much time worrying about as I was not sure it would encompass more than three days following my trial.

I do have the chance to give Rosy a hug and thank you and Corny a handshake and the same, and advise them that they are both owed what I'll never be able to repay.

I've been carefully watching over my shoulder as the group supposedly related to Morgan Tuttle has been gathering and glancing over their shoulders, talking in a manner that would make any cautious man nervous, or at least wary. And as I was informed I could pick up my personal belongings, including my weapons, but not until on the morrow, I have reason to be alarmed.

Unarmed, I'm feeling more than a bit naked. However, I'm happy to discover as we head for the gulch, Stefan Clevenger is dogging our trail and watching over the Governor and his missus, and I hope some of that protection might flow over to Mary Ann and me.

Toy's, in Helena's Last Chance Gulch, is a surprisingly fancy place, with two huge bright red carved Chinese dogs, looking more like lions than canines, flanking the entrance. A pair of doors filled with glass panes welcome us. The interior walls have life-size paintings of Chinese warriors and battle scenes. A fat Buddha statue, framed and backed up by bright red drapes, overlooks the dining area, and the kitchen is an open affair beyond. It's not connected to the restaurant unless some canvasses are pulled as ceiling between the steaming cooking area and the dining room. Behind it is the creek where gold was first discovered, which brought folks to Helena.

We take a table at the rear of the place, one with upholstered chairs. All the tables are draped with red tablecloths that hang nearly to the floor. Most have hardwood teak carved chairs, stained darkly, surrounding them. Every table, including ours, has a fancy, heavy, brass lantern at its center, and as we find our chairs, the chubby Chinese waiter lights it. A Chinese with a braided queue, black as a raven, hanging to his waist. The place is fairly dark, kept that way for atmosphere, I presume.

We are the only customers as it's midafternoon, and I wonder if the Governor has requested it so.

As we're all only a couple of hours post lunch, the Governor orders wine, beer and some snacks. Dumplings arrive with a dipping sauce that are among the most delicious things I've ever enjoyed. I have no idea what they might be stuffed with and possibly don't want to know.

The Governor toasts my freedom and we join in.

We're all smiles, until gunfire and smoke shatters our revelry.

CHAPTER 36

I CAN SEE CLEVENGER WHO HAS REMAINED BY THE FRONT
door. He's staggering backward, his arms flailing and goes
to his back. The Chinese gentleman who welcomed us
and turned us over to the waiter is trying to run in a
brocaded gown they seem to favor in dressy situations,
but it's not split up the sides far enough and he trips and
goes on his face. At first I think he too has been hit, but
the way he scrambles away like a toad with a heron on his
tail tells me no, not hit.

Two seconds after the first report I'm dragging Mary
Ann to the floor. I instruct her, "Crawl to the back, behind
that big statue." She nods, and doesn't hesitate. And I yell
to Abigale, "Follow her, stay low."

The Governor is also on the floor, half under the table
we occupy.

"You armed?" I yell at him.

"No," then he scampers on hands and knees,
following the women.

As I stay low and scamper to the side and under a

tablecloth, I'm hidden by the long drapes of red table-cloths on the dozen tables between us and the front.

Before I duck under I catch a glance of a tall fellow, sidearm in hand—one of the Tuttle clan—who kicks the fallen Clevenger in the ribs, then starts into the dining area. Still on my hands and knees, I take up a position under a table I'm sure he'll pass, and I wait. He's a disheveled sort with holes in the knees of his canvas trousers, and boots with the toes curled up a little. He's neither shaven nor bearded, but sort of half in between. The hair on the sides of his too-large head is standing straight out, as if it's carrying a lifetime of muck and dirt.

He's in no hurry, and is taking a deliberate step at a time. I'm sure he's looking from side to side hoping I'm cowering somewhere.

He draws even with me and I explode with the table in front of me like a giant war shield—and all of it in his face—and knock him backward.

Scrambling, I'm able to get a hand on the wrist of his gun hand, and we're struggling. He's a bit taller than me, which is not bad as I'm under him and have my legs under me. I lift him off his feet, but we tumble my way, and I go on my back with him over me. My right hand is free as I have his wrist in my left, and I find the brass lantern off the table I've upended and am able to smash it into the side of his head.

He screams as the fine glass chimney smashes and cuts him to the skull. He jerks away, but still has his revolver in hand. I dive and again have his wrist, then realize one of his cohorts is nearly on me. I can't react fast enough and see the butt of his rifle an instant before my lights go out.

I shake it off and come to, flat on my back, then manage to get to one knee while three equally ugly louts surround me, and I hear one cackle a little like a braying donkey.

Then he says, "Didn't want to put you in Hell until you knew who did it. That there is Clem Tuttle, I'm Tom Tuttle, and that's our cousin Elias Hawthorn. We're gonna kill you slow-like since them crooked lawyers and judge didn't see fit to stretch your neck."

All of them are holding weapons; all trained on me. As they laugh and chortle, I decide there's not a half dozen teeth in the three of them, and likely they haven't seen a bath since mama turned them loose on the world.

I don't suppose I'm going to talk my way out of this, so I might as well get a little satisfaction. "I guess you ugly louts are as crooked as that lying, scum-sucking, buggering Morgan was. Som'bitch had breath like a skunk's butt. I heard he liked little boys and was scared of women. He at least had the gumption to face me when I was heeled, a'course he had no idea I was heeled, so maybe he was just being the coward I heard all Tuttles were."

"Shut the hell up," the one who called himself Tom says. He steps forward and kicks me in the stomach. I'm on one knee, see it coming and roll with it, but it still winds me and my head is still swimming a little from the butt of the rifle. Crawling back to one knee, I'm coughing and hacking when another gunshot rocks the place, and Tom flies by me and goes to his back. I see that Clevenger is also on one knee, blood covering his chest, but with smoking revolver in hand.

Clevenger's trying to draw a bead on the other two,

but they each scramble behind separate tables. The tablecloth does one of them little good as Clevenger fans his revolver putting three quick shots through the hanging cloth, and Tuttle number two, Tom I think, goes to his back.

Then Clevenger's head goes limp, hanging, and he drops to an elbow, then to his back, seemingly out of the fight.

The one who wasn't named Tuttle, Elias I believe the one called Tom had said, rises slowly to his feet. I eyeball a revolver on the floor, one the second Tuttle dropped when he went down, but it's ten feet from me. I could dive for it were I on my feet, but on one knee ....

Elias sees me eyeing it. "Why don't you give it a try, pilgrim?" he says. He cocks his revolver and fires, but at my knee, and it burns like hell, but doesn't go out from under me. "I'm gonna kill your dumb ass a chunk at a time."

He ratchets back the hammer on the revolver again and takes a bead on my other knee, when I'm rocked by a gunshot, but not from him. He's blown over a table top and is trying to rise up when Abigale steps closer and fires again, the little Derringer she holds only has two barrels, but they're at least a .44 caliber. Mr. Elias will never stand again. Her second shot takes him under the chin as he lay across the table and relieves him of a good part of the top of his skull. He sags off the table.

I'm a bit winded but manage, "Thank you." I say it, with a smile, to the very proficient seventy-year-old woman who's just saved my bacon.

She returns the smile. "I guess that makes us even

up?" she says. And she returns the Derringer to the reticula hanging from a forearm.

"Dang tootin'," I say, and look back to see Mary Ann and the Governor at Clevenger's side. Then he walks to the front door and yells to someone to fetch a doctor.

My knee is only creased, burning like hell and will have a scar, but won't bother my dancing.

Clevenger, I see on closer inspection, is hit twice. One on his side is a through and through and unless it clipped a bowel or goes green, it won't kill him. The other is through his hip bone and he's likely to be months healing and then walk with a limp the rest of his life, if he lives.

One of the first to arrive on the scene is reporter Percy Appleseed, and the first words out of his mouth, "Killed a couple more did you? That makes, what, twenty-three or four?"

"Percy, I know this won't sell books, fact is, I'm unarmed, was busy ducking and didn't get a shot off."

"Well, hell, let's not tell it that way, Blackjack."

"Who's Blackjack?" Mary Ann asks.

"My new bodyguard," Governor Hoolihan says, and I guess I have a job, at least until Stefan Clevenger gets back on his feet. He's a hell of a man, and I hope I'm up to the task.

I can't help but turn to the Governor, "Hell, Governor, you don't need me. You got Abigale."

"True," he says, and laughs.

He's in a good mood, so I ask, "Mary Ann and I married hand-fast. I'm sure you have the power to marry official like."

"Dang tootin, I do," he says. "I didn't know you were Scottish?"

"Close enough," I say with a grin. "Then," and I turn to Mary Ann, "if it's okay with Mary Ann...how about you doing us the honor. I'm sure Mary Ann would like a certificate of some kind."

"I accept," she says, then adds, "...again," and blushes.

And she moves to me and throws her arms around my neck and plants a kiss right on my kisser.

ABOUT THE AUTHOR

L. J. Martin is the author of over three dozen works of both fiction and non-fiction from Bantam, Avon, Pinnacle and his own Wolfpack Publishing. He lives in, and loves, Montana with his wife, NYT bestselling romantic suspense author Kat Martin. He's been a horse wrangler, cook as both avocation and vocation, volunteer firefighter, real estate broker, general contractor, appraiser, disaster evaluator for FEMA, and traveled a good part of the world, some in his own ketch. A hunter, fisherman, photographer, cook, father and grandfather, he's been car and plane wrecked, visited a number of jusgados and a road camp, and survived cancer twice. He carries a bail-enforcement, bounty hunter, shield. He knows about what he writes about, and tries to write about what he knows.

OTHER WORKS BY L. J. MARTIN

Shadow of the Mast. When young Sam McCreed is shanghied he awakens aboard a California-bound hide, horn, and tallow brig. A ship he didn't want to join, on his way to a place he thought he'd never see...driven on by a vicious captain and sadistic first mate. By the time they reach the Pacific, Sam is no longer a boy but a young man hardened by ice, sea, and lash. A California that seemed a peaceful land becomes a caldron boiling over with danger and resentment. And Sam McCreed, now an expert with blade, musket, and reata, is a man on the prowl for vengeance...and he'll send any man who stands in his way straight to hell.

<u>Rush to Destiny.</u> RUSH TO DESTINY is based on the early life of the west's most quintessential hero, Edward Fitzgerald Beale. Ned Beale crossed the country horseback 13 times, he was the hero of the Battle of San Pasqual, the leader of the great camel experiment, carried the first evidence of the California gold rush to congress, fought the slave trade, was an Indian agent in California, and so much more. Beale's exploits eclipsed those of Fremont, Stockton, Custer, and even Kit Carson's, who said of Beale, "I can't believe this man, Ned Beale." My finest compliment as an author came from a California high school history teacher who said, "my students learn more California history from your book than from all their texts, ...and love doing it." Don't miss the adventures of this true hero.

<u>Unchained</u>. Jonas Cable is living exactly the life he wants...in a cabin on a lake in Montana. But a letter from a daughter he wasn't allowed to see changes all that in a heartbeat. He has a grandson he didn't know about, and his daughter pleads with him to get the 14 year old boy out of the hood. Does he owe her anything? Can he put up with a bad kid from East L.A.? And why should he change his life for someone he doesn't know and has not heard from in 30 years? And the last thing he needs is to get crossways with the L. A. gangs

Tin Angel. In this rollicking western romance, written by New York Times bestselling author Kat Martin, with husband L. J. Martin, Jessica Taggart, fresh out of a Boston finishing school, comes West...to discover the "restaurant" she's inherited from her late father is actually a saloon and bawdy house! And to add to the insult, it's run by a handsome rogue, Jake Weston, who owns 49% of Taggart Enterprises.

Myrtle Mae & The Crew. Myrtle Mae is the creation of conservative blog author L. J. Martin, and is a humorous look, as well as a serious look, a what's happening in and to our country.

<u>Blood Mountain</u>. One man ruled the mountainside - and made a deal with the would-be railroad's competitors. If Simon Striker could stop the steel tracks, he could earn a fortune. Now a brawling, quarrelling crew of immigrant railroad workers - Chinese, Irish and Polish - are about to be swept into a death trap in the mountain. And as Striker unleashes his landslide of terror, treachery and murder, a tough Irishman and sword-wielding Chinese fighter are going after him - in a battle of courage and cunning on a mountain stained with blood.

Windfall. From the boardroom to the bedroom, David Drake has fought his way...nearly...to the top. From the jungles of Vietnam, to the vineyards of Napa, to the grit and grime of the California oil fields, he's clawed his way up. The only thing missing is the woman he's loved most of his life. Now, he's going to risk it all to win it all, or end up on the very bottom where he started. This business adventure-thriller will leave you breathless.

West of the War. Young Bradon McTavish watches the bluecoats brutally hang his father and destroy everything he's known, and he escapes their wrath into the gunsmoke and blood of war. Captured and paroled, only if he'll head west of the war, he rides the river into the wilds of the new territory of Montana where savages and grizzlies await. He discovers new friends and old enemies...and a woman formerly forbidden to him.

<u>Bloodlines</u>. When an ancient document is found deep under the streets of Manhattan, no one can anticipate the wild results. A businessman is forced to search deep into his past and reach back to those who once were wronged, and redeem for them what is right and just. There's a woman he's yearned for, and must have, but all is against them...and someone wants him dead.

Repairman Series:

<u>The Repairman</u>. No. 1 on Amazon's crime list! Got a problem? Need it fixed? Call Mike Reardon, the repairman, just don't ask him how he'll get it done. Trained as a Recon Marine to search and destroy, he brings those skills to the tough streets of America's cities. If you like your stories spiced with fists, guns, and beautiful women, this is the fast paced novel for you.

<u>The Bakken</u>. No. 1 on Amazon's crime list! The stand alone sequel to The Repairman. Mike Reardon gets a call from his old CO in Iraq, who's now a VP at an oil well service company in North America's hottest boomtown, and dope and prostitution is running wild and costing the company millions, and the cops are overwhelmed. If you have a problem, and want it fixed, call the repairman...just don't ask him what he's gonna do.

G5, Gee Whiz. When a fifty million dollar G5 is stolen and flown out of the country, who you gonna call? If you have a problem, and want it fixed, call the repairman... just don't ask him what he's gonna do.

Who's On Top. Mike Reardon thinks his new gig, finding an errant daughter of a NY billionaire will be a laydown...how wrong can one guy be? She's tied up with an eco-terrorist group, who proves to be much more than that. And this time, the group he's up against may be bad guys, or kids with their heart in the right place. Who gets lead and who gets a kick in the backside. And if things go wrong, the whole country may be at risk! Another kick-ass Repairman Mike Reardon thriller from acclaimed author L. J. Martin.

Target Shy & Sexy. What's easier for a search and destroy guy than a simple bodyguard gig, particularly when the body being guarded is on of America's premiere country singers and the body is knockdown beautiful...until she's abducted while he's on his way to report for his new assignment. Who'd have guessed that the hunt for his employer would lead him into a nest of hard ass Albanians and he'd find himself between them and some bent nose boys from Vegas! Another in the highly acclaimed The Repairman Series...Mike Reardon is at it again.

Judge, Jury, Desert Fury. Back in the fray, only this time it's as a private contractor. Mike

Reardon and his buddies are hired to free a couple of American's held captive by a Taliban mullah, and, as usual, it's duck, dodge and kick ass when everyone in the country wants a piece of you. Don't miss this high action adventure by renowned author L. J. Martin. No. 6 in The Repairman series, each book stands alone.

No Good Deed. Going after some ruthless kidnappers,

who want NATO,s secrets, is one thing...going into Russia is another altogether. But when one of Reardon's crew is being held, he says to hell with it, no matter if he's risking starting World War 3! Why not add the CIA and the State Department to your list of enemies when your most important job is staying alive hour by hour, minute by minute.

Overflow. Mike Reardon, the Repairman, hates to mess his own nest—to work anywhere near where he lives. If you can call a mini-storage and a camper living. But when terrorists bomb Vegas, and a casino owner's grand-daughter is killed...the money is too good and the prey is among his most hated. Then again nothing is ever quite like it seems. Now all he has to do is stay alive, tough when friends become enemies and enemies far worse, and when you're on top the FBI and LVPD's list.

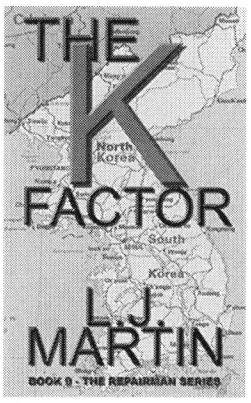

<u>The K Factor.</u>   When Mike Reardon, known as the repairman for taking jobs outside the law, is invited to a meeting with the CIA, NSA, and DOD, he knows he's about to be downrange of ka ka hitting the fan.

All they want is for him to go into North Korea and extract three women; a daughter and granddaughters of NK's ambassador to China, who wants to defect. Since he's the former head of NK's nuclear program, the U.S. is more than merely interested in him.

The Manhunter Series:

Crimson Hit
L.J. Martin
with America's No. 1 bounty hunter
Bob Burton
A Dev Shannon Novel

Crimson Hit. Dev Shannon loves his job, travels, makes good money, meets interesting people...then hauls them in cuffs and chains to justice. Only this time it's personal.

Bullet Blues. Shannon normally doesn't work in his hometown, but this time it's a friend who's gone missing, and he's got to help...if he can stay alive long enough. Tracking down a stolen yacht, which takes him all the way to Jamaica, he finds himself deep in the dirty underbelly of the drug trade.

Quiet Ops. "...knows crime and how to write about it...you won't put this one down." Elmore Leonard

L. J. Martin with America's No. 1 bounty hunter, Bob Burton, brings action-adventure in double doses. From Malibu to West Palm Beach, Brad Benedick hooks 'em up and haul 'em in...in chains.

The Clint Ryan Series:

El Lazo. John Clinton Ryan, young, fresh to the sea from Mystic, Connecticut, is shipwrecked on the California coast...and blamed for the catastrophe. Hunted by the hide, horn and tallow captains, he escapes into the world of the vaquero, and soon gains the name El Lazo, for his skill with the lasso. A classic western tale of action and adventure, and the start of the John Clinton Ryan, the Clint Ryan series.

Against the 7th Flag. Clint Ryan, now skilled with horse and reata, finds himself caught up in the war of California revolution, Manifest Destiny is on the march, and he's in the middle of the fray, with friends on one side and countrymen on the other...it's fight or be killed, but for whom?

The Devil's Bounty. On a trip to buy horses for his new ranch in the wilds of swampy Central California, Clint finds himself compelled to help a rich Californio don who's beautiful daughter has been kidnapped and hauled to the barracoons of the Barbary Coast. Thrown in among the Chinese tongs, Australian Sidney Ducks, and the dredges of the gold rush failures, he soon finds an ally in a slave, now a newly freedman, and it's gunsmoke and flashing blades to fight his way to free the senorita.

The Benicia Belle. Clint signs on as master-at-arms on a paddle wheeler plying the Sacramento from San Francisco to the gold fields. He's soon blackmailed by the boats owner and drawn to a woman as dangerous and beautiful as the sea he left behind. Framed for a crime he didn't commit, he has only one chance to exact a measure of justice and...revenge.

Shadow of the Grizzly. "Martin has produced a land-locked, Old West version of Peter Benchley's Jaws," Publisher's Weekly. When the Stokes brothers, the worst kind of meat hunters, stumble on Clint's horse ranch, they are looking to take what he has. A wounded griz is only trying to stay alive, but he's a horrible danger to man and beast. And it's Clint, and his crew, including a young boy, who face hell together.

Condor Canyon. On his way to Los Angeles, a pueblo of only one thousand, Clint is ambushed by a posse after the abductor of a young woman. Soon he finds himself trading his Colt and his skill for the horses he seeks...now if he can only stay alive to claim them.

The Montana Series – The Clan:

McCreed's Law. Gone...a shipment of gold and a handful of passengers from the Transcontinental Railroad. Found...a man who knows the owlhoots and the Indians who are holding the passengers for ransom. When you want to catch outlaws, hire an outlaw...and get the hell out of the way.

Stranahan. "A good solid fish-slinging gunslinging

read," William W. Johnstone. Sam Stranahan's an honest man who finds himself on the wrong side of the law, and the law has their own version of right and wrong. He's on his way to find his brother, and walks into an explosive case of murder. He has to make sure justice is done... with or without the law.

McKeag's Mountain. Old Bertoldus Prager has long wanted McKeag's Mountain, the Lucky Seven Ranch his father had built, and seven hired guns tried to take it the hard way, leaving Dan McKeag for dead...but he's a McKeag, and clings to life. They should have made sure...for now it will cost them all, or he'll die trying, and Prager's in his sights as well.

Wolf Mountain. The McQuades are running cattle, while running from the tribes who are fresh from killing Custer, and they know no fear. They have a rare opportunity, to get a herd to Mile's and his troops at the mouth of the Tongue...or to die trying. And a beautiful woman and her father, of questionable background, who wander into camp look like a blessing, but trouble is close on their trail...as if the McQuades don't have trouble enough.

O'Rourke's Revenge. Surviving the notorious Yuma Prison should be enough trouble for any man...but Ryan O'Rourke is not just any man. He wants blood, the blood of those who framed him for a crime he didn't commit. He plans to extract revenge, if it costs him all he has left, which is less than nothing...except his very life.

Eye For Eye. They thought his Mexican wife was a squaw...and meant only to shame, but killed instead. Quint Reagan hung up his badge, sold his ranch, and with a Smith and Wesson Russian, two Colt's, a Winchester and a coach gun went on the hunt. The Triple R had a hundred riders...but he only wanted to tack the hide of seven to the outhouse wall but the powerful owner was one of them. Sometimes revenge is the best medicine for a broken heart.

Revenge Of The Damned. A lie can be a lynchpin for a hell of a lot worse...at times it can end in a lynching! When Linc Dolan returns from the Civil War to find his former commanding officer has lied to his intended about his death in battle, and then married her, it's hell to pay. When a freak early-winter storm finds Linc wounded and sheltered in the cabin of a recently widowed home-steader and her young son, all should be fine...if he wasn't on the run from the law. Now, Bama, a black mule skinner; Twodogs, a Crow tracker; and Dolan, find themselves an unlikely gang. Damned by decent folk, hunted by the law, and pursued by Montana's most deadly man-hunters, they all three are wronged and seek bloody revenge.

The Nemesis Series:

Nemesis. The fools killed his family...then made him a lawman! There are times when it pays not to be known, for if they had, they'd have killed him on the spot. He hadn't seen his sister since before the war, and never met her husband and two young daughters...but when he heard they'd been murdered, it was time to come down out of the high country and scatter the country with blood and guts.

<u>Shadows of Nemesis.</u> When word finally reaches him that his sister and her family have died a horrid death at the hands of a cattle baron and his craven cowhands, Taggart McBain comes down off the mountain with bear traps, a double barrel coach gun, two LeMats, and a Winchester. He's on the hunt. When the task is done and blood soaks the Nemesis, NV desert, he receives a shock —his sister is still alive.

Now, with posters on every trail in Idaho and Montana territories, and a killer's price on his head, he's on the prowl. What he finds is an equal shock, but not so much as to those who hunt him. When the hunter becomes the hunted, there's pure hell to pay.

Mr. Pettigrew. Beau Boone, starving, half a left leg, at the end of his rope, falls off the train in the hell-on-wheels town of Nemesis. But Mr. Pettigrew intervenes. Beau owes him, but does he owe him his very life? Can a one-legged man sit shotgun in one of the toughest saloons on the Transcontinental. He can, if he doesn't have anything to lose.

The Ned Cody Series:

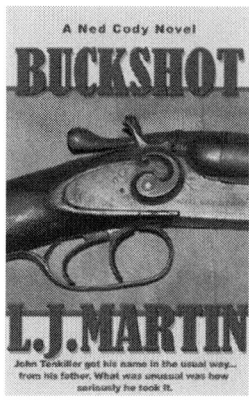

Buckshot. Young Ned Cody takes the job as City Marshal...after all, he's from a long line of lawmen. But they didn't face a corrupt sheriff and his half-dozen hard deputies, a half-Mexican half-Indian killer, and a town who thinks he could never do the job.

Mojave Showdown. Ned Cody goes far out of his

jurisdiction when one of his deputies is hauled into the hell's fire of the Mojave Desert by a tattooed Indian who could track a deer fly and live on his leavings. He's the toughest of the tough, and the Mojave has produced the worst. It's ride into the jaws of hell, and don't worry about coming back.

56020108R00152

Made in the USA
Columbia, SC
19 April 2019